POLO
COWBOY

POLO

COWBOY

a novel by
G. NERI

illustrated by
JESSE JOSHUA WATSON

CANDLEWICK PRESS

Text copyright © 2021 by G. Neri
Illustrations copyright © 2021 by Jesse Joshua Watson

First edition 2021

Library of Congress Catalog Card Number pending
ISBN 978-1-5362-0711-8

21 22 23 24 25 26 LSC 10 9 8 7 6 5 4 3 2 1

Printed in Crawfordsville, IN, USA

This book was typeset in Century Schoolbook.
The illustrations were done in pencil, clear gesso, and acrylic on bristol board, processed digitally.

Candlewick Press
99 Dover Street
Somerville, Massachusetts 02144

www.candlewick.com

A JUNIOR LIBRARY GUILD SELECTION

For Double E
GN

For Arrow
And for the youth making the changes we old folks weren't
able to yet. Don't settle for anything less than Justice for All!
JJW

ONE

Mama is fuming. "Say that again."

I swallow and take a deep breath. "I ain't goin' back to Detroit."

Five minutes ago, we was celebrating. I almost beat Harper in our first horse race—even though I'm pretty sure he let me get that close. Mama's here visiting, and we was being all family-like again, laughing and telling jokes at the Speedway in the middle of the biggest nature park in Philadelphia.

It was a great day. But then she asked me when I was gonna come back home again.

Home.

Ever since I came back to Philly to stay with my dad for the summer, I only felt one thing: *This* my home now. Where my horse, Boo, is. Where the fellas is. Where our stable, the Ritz-Carlton, is. The Ritz may have been just a run-down garage before, but to us, this barn is like the fanciest hotel in the neighborhood—the place to be and be seen—so that's why we call it that. It's my real home. Not Detroit, where Mama lives.

I didn't wanna say that out loud, but she kept asking. Now I swear her eyes is gonna drill a hole through my head.

"You the one who brung me here in the first place," I say to her stare.

It was only a year or so ago, so I know she remembers. Who forgets ditching their boy on the doorstep of a daddy he's never met?

She sighs. "I thought we had a deal. Summers here, school year back in Detroit."

Deal, schmeal. "I wanna go to school with my friends here, in Philly."

That's not exactly true. Most my friends is cowboys or small kids who come to the stables to learn. So I confess the real reason: "Besides, Boo needs me."

That don't sit right with her. "Boo's a horse," she say. "*I* need you."

"Then move back to Philly," I say. "You gettin' along with Harp now. Why can't we be a family again? In *Philly*."

I can tell that knocks her for a loop. "Life don't work that way, Cole. I can't just pick up and leave my life behind. I got a job, responsibilities. I can't just go back to a relationship that's been dead all these years. It's not that easy."

I don't wanna hurt her feelings. But truth is, I am happier here, and she knows it.

We stand there for a long time, thinking what to say next. Boo is eating grass behind me. Harper, my dad (even though I don't like to call him that), is on his horse, waiting for us to leave. I don't want Mama to go, but standing here just makes it harder to say goodbye.

"What about your future?" she asks.

"What about it?"

She sighs. "World's a tough place, Cole. Ain't got no room for young black men. You gonna end up like your cousin Smush or make something of yourself?"

I look over at Smush, who's rolling dice on the basketball court. He's a dropout and sometimes corner boy who always finding trouble, even when he's helping out.

Then I look at Harp and the other horsemen getting ready to ride back to the neighborhood. "What's wrong with bein' a cowboy?"

She almost laughs. "Being a cowboy isn't a job. Plus, it'll suck up any money you do manage to make. Just ask your dad. Your only hope is to find a way to college."

College? "Why I gotta be thinkin' about college? I'm only fourteen. What's that gotta do with stayin' here?"

She glances over at Harp. "I'm not so sure your dad is thinking about your future. He's not even thinking about his own."

I stare at the ground for the longest time, trying to find the words. I wanna tell her I love her, that this ain't got nothing to do with the past.

Instead what comes out is "Maybe, but I still wanna stay in Philly."

She stares at me like she trying to read my mind, like she trying to see if I really feel that way or if I'm just being a teenager.

Then she laughs, but not in a funny way. "You just like your daddy. Love that horse more than me."

4

She turns to leave, and it feels like she just put a knife in my back. "Wait," I say.

She stops, shakes her head. I grab her from behind. She sighs and pulls me into a bear hug till I can't breathe. "I love you too," she says.

Then she walks away before we both lose it.

TWO

I need to get my head together.

Am I sure about this? *Move to Philly for real?* I ain't even asked Harp about this yet. I just been playing it out in my head.

"Looks like you two had words," says Harp, like he's had a word or two with her hisself.

I nod, but I ain't ready to get into it. "I'm sure you'll hear all about it before she head back tonight." I expect more grilling, but Harp don't say nothing.

"You mind if I take Boo out?" I ask.

He sees I don't wanna talk. "See ya back at the Ritz."

. . .

Whenever things get too much for me, I escape deep
into Fairmount Park. This is me and Boo's favorite
place. You can wander for miles, escape all the noise
of the city, and just disappear into that forest—riding
alone, listening to the leaves in the wind or the sound
of the creek trickling by. Whenever I come here, I
forget all my troubles and feel whole again.

I don't wanna sound corny or nothing, but Boo is,
like, my best friend now. I can tell him anything and
he don't judge.

"I don't know why she trippin'. I kept up my end
of the deal. Passed eighth grade. Stayed outta trouble.
Am I right?"

Boo don't say nothing, which feels like a *"Right."*

"Principal even shook my hand and said, 'I wasn't
sure you could do it, but you made it.' Mama should be
happy."

Boo kinda nods . . . but he do that when he walks.

"Maybe I can make a *new* deal. Maybe switch it
around and spend the *summer* in Detroit and the rest
of the year here? Whatchou think about that?"

Boo stops and looks back at me.

I know a guilt trip when I see one. "Don't you give
me a hard time too, Boo. I know it sucked when I was

7

gone. You don't think I know what it feels like to be abandoned? I *know*."

I let out a sigh, then look around to see where we are. There's a clearing up ahead where I can see the end of a metal fence. When we get up close, I see it's a corral fence.

Then it hits me.

"Oh, dang, Boo. You know what this is? It's that police barn I broke you out of."

His ears rise up in high alert. I can feel his body tense. I wonder if he really remembers that week when the city inspectors took him away and locked him and the other horses up in here. He musta been so scared, just like I was when I watched them cart him away. Seem like a million years ago when we busted them out in the middle of the night and hid in the park like we was train robbers in the Old West.

"Easy, Boo," I say, looking around. "Somethin' looks different."

What's different is that the whole place is emptied out like a ghost town. We trot around the edge of the corral till we come to the barn. But there ain't no horses. No people. No equipment. Nothing.

"Looks like they moved out." I get down and walk Boo around. I try the main barn door, but it's locked. I peek in through the crack. With most barns, the smell of horses hits you, and it's like being home. Here, nothing.

Empty.

"Man, they really is gone. Good—no more horsenappers!" I karate-kick the gate to the corral, and it opens. "Boo, check it out! Wanna go for a spin?"

I lead him into the corral, then chase him till he's galloping around in circles along the fence. We play tag for a bit, but he keeps running long after I'm outta breath.

I climb on top a the fence and watch him. He looks happy. Running here ain't like running around the empty lot across from our stable, which is full of holes, weeds, and broken glass. This is like real dirt that has been taken care of.

Boo peters out and stops at a trough with some rainwater in it. I pet his neck, and he gets his drink on. "Man, imagine if we lived here, Boo. Wouldn't that be dope? You could sleep in that barn in style and run out here every day. *That*'d be livin'."

I feel for Boo—his stable is dark and old and made up from broken doors and scrap plywood, and the air is thick with dust and cobwebs, and sometimes there's even rats running around. Being here feel like . . . heaven.

I'm sitting there dreaming what I could do with the place when I hear some kinda strange noise.

Thwack—bang!... Thwack—bang!... Thwack—bang!

What's that?

I leave Boo at the trough and follow the sound out the corral. It seem to be coming from the other side of the barn.

The barn is big, so it takes me a few minutes to walk around its edges. The sound is getting louder, and then, when I come up on a corner, I start hearing a voice too. A girl's voice, counting.

Thwack—bang!... "Twenty-two."

Thwack—bang!... "Twenty-three."

When I peek around the corner, I see the weirdest thing: a girl sitting on a sawhorse with a piece of cardboard for a saddle, holding the reins like it's a real horse or something. She's hitting red softballs with a long wood hammer.

She takes a swing at one of them balls—*thwack!* It sails through the air and hits a square chalked on the side of the barn—*bang!*

"Twenty-four," she counts.

I have no idea what she's doing, but I watch her hit a few more. She's dressed funny too—wearing a helmet and on her arms and knees is leather pads. On her feet she's wearing long black boots that cover her calves. She got on white pants and a dark shirt that says one word: CHUKKERHEAD.

When she runs outta balls, she climbs down offa that thing and starts collecting the loose ones in a basket. But then she puts the basket at the foot of her "horse" and takes off her helmet—

Oh—*dang.*

She about my age, but her face—it looks like she's made up for Halloween or something. Her skin is dark, like mine. But around her eyes, nose, and mouth is painted like . . . *white.*

Like she just dipped the front of her head into a bowl of paint or something.

"It's not polite to stare," she says suddenly.

I look around and realize she talking to me.

"I wasn't starin'," I say (even though I was). "I mean, I just heard a noise and came around to check it out."

She looking at me, but the whole mask thing is freaking me out, 'cause it ain't paint. It's her *skin.* I try to change the subject.

"What happened to the mounted police?" I ask. "I mean, last time I was here, they kept all a their horses in the stable."

11

She dumps the basket of balls. "They're gone. Closed the program."

"Really? Why?"

She climbs back up on her wood horse. "Mom says it cost the city too much to feed them and clean up after them."

She aims and takes a swing at a ball. *Thwack— bang!* . . . "Twenty-six."

"I think you was on twenty-five," I say.

She ignores me, but on the next hit—*Thwack— bang!*—she says *"Twenty-six!"* with attitude.

I watch her take a few more whacks. "What're you doin'?" I ask.

"What's it look like? Practicing my half-seat trunk rotation."

"Your what?"

She laughs. "Polo, dummy."

Only polo I know is them shirts some kids wear around. "Like . . . Ralph Lauren Polo?"

She stops and looks at me like I'm stupid. "If you gonna stand there, make yourself useful. Get those balls for me, will you?"

I don't know why, but I do it. I hustle over to where a couple balls sit near the barn wall. "Can I ask you a question?"

Thwack! A ball sails by, just missing my head. *BANG!*

"Hey!" I shout.

She stares me down, hard, then points to her face. "It's called vitiligo, if you gotta know," she says. "It's a disease that causes the loss of skin color. So, *no*, I'm not dressed like a clown for Halloween, and I'm not part Dalmatian. *Okay?*"

I pick up the balls and walk over to where she is and dump them. "I was just gonna ask you what a chukkerhead is," I say.

She kinda laughs like she ain't sure if I'm lying or not. Finally she says, "A chukkerhead is anyone who loves polo."

"I never seen anyone play polo except for a polo game I saw on TV once. But it was in a pool, and there weren't no wood horses or hammer sticks," I say. "I did play Marco Polo once, but that was in a pool too."

Now she just looks sorry for me. "Are you, like, simple in the head or something? And by the way, these aren't hammer sticks. They're called mallets and—"

She suddenly stops talking and her expression changes. I hear Boo amble up behind me. He starts nibbling at the back of my head.

"That your pony?" she asks.

I take his reins and climb up till I'm eye level with her. "He's a horse, not a pony. His name is Boo," I say.

Boo don't seem to care, 'cause he goes right up to her like he knows her. "Hey, Boo . . ." she says, like they old friends.

I interrupt their moment with a little dig. "So, what's *your* horse's name?"

She looks at her wooden ride, with a makeshift saddle on it. "We call them ponies in polo." She thinks. "I think his name is . . . Woody. So, you a rider, then? Boo belongs to *you*?"

She seems surprised for some reason, so I set her straight. "I'm a cowboy, I guess. From over on Chester Avenue?"

She nods. I try not to stare at her, but being face-to-face, it's hard not to. "You know what's gonna happen to the barn?" I ask, trying to change the subject.

She shrugs. "I dunno. Seems stupid to let it go to waste, though. I been using it to practice. Nobody bothers me here." She's looking at Boo, and then acts like a light bulb went off in her head. "Hey, you wanna scrimmage?"

"'Scrimmage'?" I'm not sure what she means or that I wanna spend any more time here. "Uh, not today. I kinda hafta get goin' now."

She nods, looking at Boo. "Well, next time. We'll go one-on-one. Boo likes it."

I don't know why she talking about Boo like they go way back, but it's getting on my nerves. "Whatever," I say. I pull on Boo's reins and back him out to show her what I can do.

"See you when I see you," she says.

"Not if I see you first," I say.

THREE

I got too much on my mind to think about that crazy black girl with the white face—like convincing Harp to let me stay the year with him in Philly.

Harp is moody, so I gotta find the right time to hit him up. He's most calm when he's brushing down his horse, Lightning, on the sidewalk outside our barn while the other fellas hang out on Chester Ave., jawing and telling jokes. I find him there.

"You talk to Mama?" I ask.

"More like she talked to me," he says.

I wait for more, but it ain't coming. "So . . . what you think, then?" I finally ask. "I mean, about me stayin' an' all?"

He keeps brushing. "Wished you woulda asked me first. Then I coulda said no up front."

Dang.

"Sorry. It just kinda came up," I say. "So . . . you don't want me to stay?"

He don't answer, just keeps brushing. But then he says, "It's just . . . I didn't see it coming."

I let that sink in. "I thought I could maybe go to high school in the neighborhood," I say. "And take care of Boo, you know, full-time." I pick up the hose and start rinsing off Lightning. Harp stands back and watches. "You know—so you don't have to," I add.

He takes out a cigarette, lights it. "Might wanna think twice about going to high school here. It's kind of gone downhill since my day, just like this neighborhood."

"You went to North?" I ask. North is the only high school around.

"Yeah. It was all right. Played football. But I heard they had to close down the sports program 'cause other teams were too afraid to come here."

"To come *here*? What's wrong with here?"

He clears his throat. "Nothing, if you in the right gang."

That don't shake me. If it was good enough for him, should be okay for me.

He's thinking on it, and I let him. Trying to convince him is like convincing a cat to play fetch. I watch him as he takes off his favorite bandanna and washes it gently in the bucket. Sometime it feel like he likes that rag more than me. "Your mama said that if you stayed, I'd have to take a more 'active role' in your future." He eyes me like he just noticed I've grown two inches this summer. "What do you think you might want to do after school is done? And don't say cowboyin'."

I shrug. "I don't know. I'm fourteen, remember? What'd you wanna be when you was fourteen?"

He laughs. "I wanted to be starting wide receiver for the Eagles. Didn't work out."

"Well, I don't know, then," I say. "I just wanna be able to keep Boo and ride him when I want."

He grunts, then starts brushing Lightning again without answering.

"So . . . can I stay?" I ask. "I mean, for school. I'll do good, I promise. And I'll call them and find out everythin' I gotta do to transfer."

He sighs. "Listen. You wanna stay here? You gotta pull your load. That means you gotta get a job."

A job? Now he's just playing me. "But . . . I'm only fourteen."

He looks at me dead in the eye, like, *So what?*

"I had my first job at nine."

Not sure I believe him. "Doin' what?"

"Working my daddy's stable."

"I already do that," I say.

"I mean for money. Ain't nobody got no money here for you. You gotta go where the money's at. Some people pay good money for a young'un who knows how tack, feed, muck, and exercise a horse."

"Yeah, you know some rich horse people?"

He's staring at me now, sizing me up. I seen that look before, and no good comes of it. "I just might know someone."

FOUR

Even at dawn, when the sunrise casts a pretty orange glow over Chester Avenue, our neighborhood looks run-down. I mean, I ain't complaining. It's home for now, and we make do with what we got. Vacant garage? Turn it into a stable, using old plywood, doors, whatever. Empty lot becomes a corral. Boarded-up house? Expand your crib, like Harp done by taking over the place next door (and by putting a hole in the wall for a door). Add a bedroom for your son by kicking out the horse you had living inside there.

I don't know why I let Harp get me up so early on a Saturday, but a deal's a deal (his words) and I gotta pay the piper (again, his words). He has a job for me, and in the past, that meant driving up to Bucks County, where the Amish live and raise horses. We go up there to buy feed or gear or check out a auction or two. So, I figure I'll be loading stuff for some Amish dude all morning.

But when we driving, instead of going up the interstate outta Philly, we cross the bridge *over* the highway into Fairmount Park.

"Where we goin'?" I yawn. I ain't eaten or had juice or nothing, but I figure we'll stop along the way and grab something.

"You'll see," he grunts.

I know that game. When he says "You'll see," that mean he don't wanna get into it. He'll just spring it on me and leave me before I can complain.

I stare out the window at the park passing me by. "We goin' to the Speedway?"

"Not today."

"Okay . . ." I know better than to push too much. We driving straight across the park now, past the tennis courts and pool, over the river to where there are wide-open green pastures and the rich people like

to sun themselves and have picnics. They get mad at us sometimes when we ride through and disturb their goings-on.

Soon, we at the other end of the park, and I see a big fancy sign on a fancy brick wall that surrounds a fancy neighborhood.

WELCOME TO THE HEIGHTS.

"What are we doin' here?" I ask. The Heights is the opposite of our neighborhood, Strawberry Mansion.

They shoulda called *this* part Mansion, 'cause that's all that's here: big houses with giant, perfect lawns, long driveways, and expensive cars. Some even got their own tennis courts.

As we drive, the Heights starts to open up, and the properties get bigger. It's more country feeling than Philly. "Dang, look. They got horses." I point to some big-ass property with a white fence and expensive-looking horses galloping freely across a open field.

"Someday . . ." he says.

Right. When we hit the lotto. I gaze out at them horses. Man, that would be the life.

We turn onto a leafy street, and there's a even bigger property that has a buncha white-brick buildings with Roman columns like you see in the movies. There's even some cannons facing out over the green hills.

"Man, somebody got too much money," I say.

"Well, hopefully they'll pay a decent wage for a kid who ain't never had a proper job."

He points to a sign at the head of a long driveway. GEORGE WASHINGTON MILITARY ACADEMY.

What the—? Suddenly, I realize I been scammed. "Stop the car!"

He shakes his head, grinning. "Relax, Cole. I ain't shipping you off to military school. Least not yet."

I stare daggers at him. I can't tell if he's serious or not. "You better be jokin'."

He pulls up and stops at the foot of the driveway. About a hundred feet along is a iron gate reaching for the sky. Two dudes in military outfits stand alert behind the fence, looking at us.

"So, why we stoppin', then?" I ask.

Harp pulls out a piece of paper and hands it to me. All it says is *Coach Whitman.*

"What am I supposed to do with this?" I ask.

"Tell the cadets you're looking for the stables. They'll be expecting you."

I stare at him. "You gonna have to say more than that to get me outta this truck."

He turns to me. "I pulled some strings, called in a favor. At least it's not McDonald's. You'll be using your horse skills."

24

I look at him, unsure, but horsing sounds better than flipping burgers. "Why don't you come with me, then?"

"You'll be fine," he says, starting the engine again. "I got places to be. Out."

I get out and watch him drive off. I got my jeans and T-shirt, boots, and cowboy hat on. As I walk up the driveway, I notice the words COURAGE, HONOR, SUCCESS set into the gate. The two soldiers look at me, then each other, then me again. They not making me feel too welcome.

I stop in front of the gate, and one of them holds up his hand. "Can I help you, sir? You have business here?"

I realize these ain't soldiers. They kids *pretending to be* soldiers. "Yeah, if it's any of your concern."

I hand him the piece of paper. The kid soldier looks at it, then shows it to his partner. "What am I supposed to do with this?"

I wanna tell him what he can do with it, but I don't. "I'm expected. At the stables."

"Stables?" the shorter one says. "We have stables?"

The taller one nods without taking his eyes off me. "Yeah. On the south end of campus. But we sure as heck don't have any cowboys there. That's C Troop—cavalry unit."

"Oh," says the other. "Cool. They have sabers and stuff?"

"Better believe it," says the tall one. "Cut this cowpoke right in half. *Sliiice.*" He acts out doing just that.

I've had enough. "Look, guys, as much as I'd love to sit here and listen to you toy soldiers, you better call it in or whatever you have to do, 'cause I'm comin' in whether you like it or not. I got orders."

The short one looks surprised. "From the commander?"

I shake my head. "A higher authority. My dad."

Five minutes later, the shorter boy is escorting me to the stables. His partner said he has permission to shoot to kill if I get out of hand, but I think he was joking.

He keeps looking at me like he wants to ask me something. Finally, he says, "Are you a plebe?"

I stop. "What did you call me?" I'm about to get all up in his face when he suddenly stands at attention and salutes someone approaching us.

I turn, and another student in a fancier blue military uniform and beret is coming up on us. He can't be all of seventeen, but the kid acts like a general is approaching.

"At ease, plebe," says the fancy guy, who hasn't even started shaving yet. "What do we have here?" He looks me up and down like *I'm* the one dressed funny.

"Escorting this . . . gentleman to the stable, sir."

He shakes his head, like he don't approve. "You must be the new stable boy."

"I know you didn't just call me boy, *son*," I say.

"That's the *first lieutenant*," the other one whispers at me. "He's our platoon leader."

"I don't care if he's Cap'n Crunch. I'm nobody's boy—"

The first lieutenant smiles. "Just an expression, sir. Stable boy, stable hand, groom. Same thing."

But I can see through him. He means *boy*. I laugh it off. "You probably don't know a halter from a bridle."

The first lieutenant smiles. "Oh, I see we have a real horseman here. I didn't know your kind knew how to ride proper."

"My kind?" I'm about to show him my kind.

He nods and starts on his way. "I mean you cowboys. Good thing you'll be working here. Maybe you'll learn something new. And by the way, at least I know a chukker from an inning, which is more than you can say."

I let it go. Maybe I'm reading too much into him.

"Don't expect me to call you Lieutenant," I say. "I'm not one of you."

"Well, if you don't want to call me that . . ." he says over his shoulder, "then call me Maverick. That's my name in the arena."

The cadet looks at me, surprised I stood up to the fancy kid, and maybe gives me a little more respect. We keep making our way across campus. I spot some other cadets dressed in black, breaking into a slow sprint— slow only because they're hauling instruments: tuba, drums, trumpets. My cadet sees me watching.

"Morning formations," he says.

I see the cadets fall into line as Maverick walks up to them.

"At-ten-*tion!*" someone calls out. They line up in two perfect lines, frozen in salute for the first lieutenant. Weird.

We keep moving away from the action. Across a parking lot, across a field with a track, across what looks like a military boot camp obstacle course.

"You gonna go fight a war or somethin'?" I ask.

He shrugs. "Me? I want to do cybersecurity. After college, of course."

"You already thinkin' of college?" I ask. "How old are you?"

"Thirteen." He shakes off my first question. "Everyone here goes to college," he says, matter-of-fact.

I notice we're heading into the woods. But there's a hidden staircase going down a hill, and when we hit a clearing, I see it: a huge barn and stables.

"Dang. That's big," I say to myself.

"I never been down here before. That thing is full of horses?" the cadet asks, pointing at the big barn. But it ain't like no barn I ever seen. First of all, it looks like it's three stories tall. We walk past a couple corrals, and I step up to a side entrance of the barn and peek in.

Inside is a giant arena surrounded by bleachers. It's one giant empty room with a sandy dirt floor and all kinds of horse obstacles inside.

"Move it, *plebes!*"

I turn around and two dudes—teens—wearing funny-looking leather armor barge past us on horses. They got on blue polo shirts and helmets and knee-high black boots and is carrying wooden mallets like that girl had in the park. They look like they come off one of those Ralph Lauren ads. The guys eye me suspiciously like I'm some country hick. The one closest to me, a big lean white dude with flaming red hair and eyebrows, uses his mallet to knock my hat off my head.

"Hey! Try that again, man—" I shout.

He brings his horse back around until the horse is in my face. "Or what, *plebe?*"

I can see he'd like to run me over. He's big, and his horse is bigger, sixteen hands at least. But I'm from North Philly. "Or I'll take that mallet and—"

"You Cole?" I hear someone shout out from across the way. I look over and see a small dark-haired woman dressed in horse gear.

"Yeah," I say, looking at Big Red. He shakes his head and moves into the arena. "Next time," I hear him mutter.

I sneer at him as he passes. I wave to the lady. "Comin'."

I nod to my cadet, who seems in awe of the horses. "Yo, I'm good now. You can head back if you like. What's your name?

"PFC Johnson, sir. Though technically I'm still a plebe."

"What's with all this 'plebe' stuff?"

"That's what they call all first-year cadets. Until Recognition Day. Then you become private first class. And after a year, you get to be called an Old Man! I can't wait to be old." He sees I have no idea what he's talking about. "Um, but my civilian name is Ronnie."

I make a face. "For real?"

"I'm afraid so."

He salutes me, then runs off but keeps stopping every few steps to watch the horses in action. I watch them too as I head toward the woman.

"Nice horses you got here. Coach Whitman?" I ask, extending my hand.

"We call them ponies, but, yeah, they keep us busy." She shakes my hand; she's small but strong. Her green eyes take me in. "So, you're Harp's son?"

I nod. I hope that's a good thing. "Well, lucky for you, we're short-staffed. My foreman got another job, so he can only help in the mornings on weekdays. Need someone for weekday afternoons and Saturday mornings to tack and barn the animals. Exercise and groom, wrap and braid, keep the tack clean and organized, muck, feed, tack up the ponies for workouts and matches. The usual."

"Braid?" I ask, trying not to act like I ain't never heard of that, 'cause I ain't.

She nods toward a pony with its shaved mane and tail braided tight. "You never played polo?"

I clear my throat. "I can ride faster than almost anyone here. Do barrel racing, jumps. But . . . no, not . . . polo."

She nods. "Harp says you're a fast learner."

"He said that?" I say, surprised. "Um, I don't gotta wear no uniform around here, do I?"

She sees me looking at the big dude's uniform. "No, Cole. That's for cadets only. You just need to focus on the horses. Ignore everything else. You ever exercise multiple ponies at once? It's like being a dog walker, except with ponies walking alongside you in a row."

"No, ma'am. But if they're used to it, I can figure it out. When can I start?"

She laughs. "Now. You're starting now. Didn't he tell you?"

"Not really. And, um, what about pay?"

She sighs. "Technically, you're a bit young to be on staff, but as a favor to Harp, we'll see how it goes, keep it off the books for now. Harp's debt will be forgiven, and we'll be square."

"Wait—his 'debt'? I ain't gettin' paid?"

She considers her words. "You'll have to talk to him. But if I were you, I'd take the deal. Who knows? You might even learn something."

I work only a few hours at the Academy that morning. It's enough. I learn that C Troop, the cavalry unit, is made up of a coupla different groups of cadets—the polo players, dressage riders (that funny prancing horsing you see on TV), and a few other guys who ride in parades. I'm supposed to help take care of all the horses, plus help the polo players with other jobs. I keep my eye on three of the players, including that Maverick dude and Big Red, riding around the ring in weird formations—all in a row, breaking into figure eights, stopping and starting, turning on a dime. Feels like they're showing off.

The polo crew treat me like I'm their personal stable boy. They dump all their gear into a pile and tell me to sort and clean it—including shining their boots. "And you better see your reflection in them," says Maverick.

Coach says the barn is like their second home, so they like to hang out after practice. For entertainment, they watch me as I try to halter and rope five ponies into a line so I can take them for a twenty-minute trot. Maverick sees me struggling, so he gives me a piece of advice: "Ponies are like sheep. Everything they do, they do as a unit, and *you* are their shepherd. You just gotta lead 'em and they'll follow."

What he don't tell me is that there's a pecking order to these ponies, and if you get them in the wrong order, they don't act like sheep but like dogs with attitudes, moving every which way but straight ahead.

The ponies have themselves a good ol' time at my expense.

After the others leave, the smallest guy of the three, a squirrelly-looking kid with deep gray eyes and a slight southern accent, apologizes, saying it was a tradition to razz the new kids. Then he asks me if I have anything on me.

"Like what?" I ask, confused.

He looks around. "You know . . . weed, or whatever?"

I stare at him for a long beat. "Do I . . . look like a drug dealer?"

He just shrugs. "You're a brother from the 'hood, ain't ya?"

"I'm fourteen," I tell him. "You should leave."

He holds up his hands. "Okay, I get it. First day, make a good impression. But after you're settled awhile, you'll hook a brother up, right?"

I don't answer. Just look at that pile of gear and think of quitting right then and there.

FIVE

When I wake up, it's still dark out. Harp is standing over me. He don't say nothing—just waits for me to realize I gotta get up. I know he won't move till I do, so I do.

I sit on the edge of my bed and realize what day it is. First day of high school. First day of school in Philly. My first day of classes *not* in Detroit.

For a minute, I picture Mama making me breakfast, like she did most a my life. Cereal. Toast. OJ. Sometimes a egg or two. She would pack my lunch the way I like: PB&J sandwich on white with sliced bananas, no crust. Chips (BBQ). Fruit roll (cherry). Drink (Yoo-hoo).

I wonder for a second if she'll do that this morning before she realizes I'm not there.

I get up, wander over to the kitchen. Harp is already gone. No breakfast, no lunch, nothing.

The fridge is empty except for some beer and leftover pizza. I stare at it and count back how many days old that pizza is. Too old.

I know Harp is at the stable, so I throw my jeans on and wander over. Sure enough, him and his two right-hand men, Tex and Jamaica Bob, are already mixing feed and raking up crap.

Tex looks up at me through his Coke-bottle glasses and smiles. "The prince awakes. I don't believe I've ever seen you up this early before."

"School day," I say, all grumpy.

His eyes light up. "School! Damn. What grade you going into, son?"

"Ninth."

"Ninth?" Bob pipes up. "The formative years." He chuckles, tying his long dreads into a knot.

"'Course, I never made it to ninth," says Tex. "But I hear it's when the girls start coming on to ya."

They share a good laugh. "You never went to high school?" I ask, like that's a option.

"Had to work, son. My daddy left us, so it was just

me being the man of the house. 'Sides, what do I need prom fer? I already had all the ladies lining up when I rode my Daisy around."

"Ha. You mean one-eyed Daisy?" says Bob. "All that horse ever attracted was flies. Me, on the other hand: Prom king. Star quarterback. Valedictorian—"

"Were all people you *met* in class," says Harper. "You? You were just listening to reggae on your Discman morning, noon, and night."

I turn to Harper. "And how'm I supposed to do good in school if we ain't got nothin' to eat? Mama always made me breakfast *and* lunch."

Tex and Bob exchange glances.

Harp spits. "I'm not your mother. Besides, you qualify for free breakfast and lunch at school, so I suggest you take it up with them and save us the hassle of shopping. Money's tight."

Really? "I thought I was payin' for room and board," I say.

He hands me his rake. "And Boo's too. Better get busy so you can finish and get that free breakfast before class."

Him and the others leave me be. I feel Boo breathing down my neck. I turn and he licks my shoulder from his stall. "Guess you the only one who's glad to see me these days." I hug his neck, and he rests his jaw on my back. I stay like that for a good long time.

"Well, well, look who it is." My first greeting at North High School is from Harp's cop friend, Leroy, who's manning the metal detector.

"You get demoted?" I ask.

"Funny. I'm helping out. First day is always a little crazy. Empty your pockets, Cole."

"I got nothin' in my pockets," I say.

He sees me holding a pencil. "Where's your backpack at?" he asks.

I shrug. "Don't have one."

He eyes me. "So, you come to school on the first day and all you got is a *pencil*?" he says. I start to notice everyone else has a backpack and notebooks. He sees me looking, then shakes his head. "Just tell Harper he needs to go shopping for school supplies, ya hear?" he says quietly.

I can barely hear him. In front of me is a sea of kids, wall-to-wall, laughing and shouting like they all know each other and been friends all they life. Me? I know no one at this school. All my friends are horses or old heads like Tex or young'uns like Lil'

C-Jay or dropouts like my cousin Smush. All my real friends I left behind in Detroit.

I walk through the detector. It goes off. Leroy pulls me aside. "You have any metal on you? Better not be a weapon."

"I ain't packin'." I pull up my shirt to reveal the brass buckle on my belt, the one Tex gave me last year. It says GHETTO COWBOY on it.

He smiles. "Nice. How're things on Chester Ave.? Still causing riots?"

"Just keepin' it real."

"Uh-huh. You're not gonna raise any ruckus here, are ya?" He's only half kidding.

I ignore him. "Is this thing gonna go off every time I walk through?"

He nods. "It's how it is." He waves me through. "I recommend you don't wear a belt. At least not one with a buckle like that. See you on the trail, maybe."

Thirty seconds after I step out into all the hustle, someone shoves me from behind and my face smacks into a locker. Two girls is going at it, and someone knocked me over, trying to get a better look at the fight. Whistles blow; phones whip out. I watch as Leroy and a woman who seems like the principal tear the two apart. All kind of cuss words fill the air as camera phones are held up high to catch the action.

"You bleeding," some girl says to me. I feel my lip and see blood on my fingers.

First morning in, and I'm already wondering if it's too late to go back home.

SIX

By the time I walk out of school, I feel like a old man. Classrooms that are supposed to fit twenty-five got thirty-five kids in them. I had to sit on the floor for two of 'em, on a old plastic milk crate in another. I noticed a dead cockroach next to me, and that's pretty much how I felt on my first day. No windows neither, and 'cause it's like eighty degrees out, it hot and stuffy too.

Breakfast and lunch coulda technically been called food, but I'm pretty sure the FDA might not agree. Burger looked like it was frozen since the ice age, taters overcooked and cold, and I had a Twinkie that I swear expired eight months ago—and that's saying something. But since I was starving, I scarfed it all down, and now my stomach feels like it got something dead in there.

Nobody talked to me all day except a coupla teachers who gave me attitude for not having the right supplies. The principal, who I guess is new here, was handing out #ANewDayIsDawningAtNorth stickers, then warned us not to stick them on the school. And, oh yeah, I got cornered by the 29th Street Disciples 'cause someone told 'em I live on Chester Ave. and they think I'm Chester Ave. Cobras. So all I wanna do is go home and sleep.

That's when I see Harp in his truck, sitting at the curb in front. And something tells me he ain't just giving me a ride home.

He nods at me and starts the engine before I even get in. I slide into the passenger seat, and it feels like I could just fall asleep right there. He pulls out.

No *How was your day? How was school?* or *I remember when I went here* stories. Just driving. I can see we ain't going home. We heading across the park again. And we're not riding or he'd be on Lightning with Boo in tow. Then I get it.

"Payin' off your debt?" I ask.

"Working. And it's *your* debt."

"My debt?" I say. "I don't remember borrowin' any money."

"Well, while you were away last year, who do you think took care of Boo?" he says.

I thought it was him. But then I put two and two together. "You mean, you left him at the *Academy*?"

He nods, matter-of-fact. "I heard they were short on ponies, and those stables are better than ours. I was too busy with work to take care of horses that aren't mine. At least there, he was eating and getting workouts."

The idea of those cavalry boys on Boo makes my skin crawl. "Are you tellin' me you let those damn cadets use Boo? And now we gotta *pay* for it?"

"Actually, *you* gotta pay for it. Babysitting ain't free."

I sit and stew on that the whole way in.

He drops me at the gate again, but this time it's open and there are no guards staring me down. I remember the way, so I wander up that long driveway, past the massive lawns and cannons and the brick building with columns.

I look up at the windows and see students in classrooms. A teacher with glasses is watching me as I move past. Off in the distance, I see a squadron marching in step like you see in the movies.

This sure ain't like North High. They don't got metal detectors and fights breaking out, and probably they got small classes where everyone gets a desk. I bet they got good food too. For a second, I imagine me sitting up in one of those rooms with my own desk and school supplies, my fancy threads on, wondering if I should have steak for lunch—

"You got a reason to be here?"

I turn around, and it's a cop. Not no kid cop neither. A big, buff, hard-ass cop. And he's looking at me.

My mama taught me never to talk back to the police. We had a friend who was killed by 5-0 two years ago on a random stop. But I remind myself that I have a reason to be here.

"Yeah, I do." I look at him, and for some reason I just can't help adding, "Is it against the law to walk while black here?"

He tilts his head, and I see his left hand casually unsnap his baton. "It is if you're trespassing."

I sober up quick. "I work here," I say. "Someone report me?"

He seems doubtful. "You have some kind of ID? A work pass?"

I don't have a driver's license or nothing, and school just started, so I don't have ID yet. "I work down at the stables."

"Stables, huh? Maybe you and me should take a ride down there."

"I'm good. I can walk."

But next thing I know, I'm sitting in the back of a police car behind a cage. This is not what I signed up for. We pull up to the stables, and I see the cadets staring at me from the outside corral.

Great.

I sit in the back as the two polo kids from before—Big Red and the squirrelly one—watch the action while they saddle their ponies. Some of the other C Troop cadets are there too, just hanging out, it seems. The cop talks to Coach Whitman, who looks alarmed. The cavalry point at me and joke around at my expense. Finally, Coach hustles over and lets me out.

"I'm so sorry, Cole. I'll get you a laminated badge for next time. We had some intruders recently, so we were told to report any strangers on campus. Please don't take it personally."

I don't say nothing, just step out the car and watch the cop get back in. He don't say nothing either. But the big kid does. "Nice ride, stable boy."

Before I can say *Don't call me boy*, Coach interrupts. "Gentlemen, this is Cole. Have you forgotten the rule of C Troop in regard to visitors?"

They look at each other like they know where this is going. "He's not a visitor. He's a worker," says the squirrelly kid. "Besides, I heard he's from Strawberry

Mansion. That place is all thugs and gangbangers."

I look at him and wanna say *Like you know*, but I don't.

Coach walks up to them all calm-like and looks at the big kid with the red hair. He sighs, then stands and says, "The rule of C Troop in regard to visitors is to always salute and show respect."

Then he salutes me like it's the hardest thing he ever had to do and waits for the others to follow. They sigh, rise up, and offer a half-hearted salute. "Good afternoon, sir."

"That wasn't so painful, was it?" says Coach Whitman. "Cole, I'm going to make you a badge. You assist these gentlemen in their exercises today, okay?"

"Yes, ma'am."

We all watch Coach as she disappears into the barn. "At ease, boys," I say as a joke. They don't laugh.

The polo dudes look me up and down as they walk around me in a circle. Then one of them sees Maverick coming out the barn. He's dressed like the others, not in a uniform but ready to work out. And not in a good mood.

"Atten-*tion!*" shouts Big Red, and the others stand and salute.

Maverick barely salutes back but stops when he sees me. "Well, well. Look who we have here."

Big Red goes over and whispers in his ear. Maverick cracks a smile, never taking his eyes off me. He says something back to Big Red, who salutes as Maverick heads into the arena.

Big Red lowers his gaze on me and grins, not in a good way. "The first lieutenant requests your help in our workout." He points to the equipment. "See that wagon full of sticks and balls? Why don't you pull it into the arena, and we'll show you how things run around here, okay, stable boy?"

He salutes me, but it feels more like a setup than a sign of respect.

SEVEN

Next thing I know, the squirrelly kid, Big Red, and that First Lieutenant Maverick are in the arena, staring me down, their ponies behind them. The ponies' manes are shaved, their tails are braided, and they're wearing shin guard things like the ones soccer players wear. The guys look like mercenaries: helmets, goggles, leather elbow pads and kneepads, high shiny black boots, clean white pants, and bright-blue polo practice shirts.

Maverick points at me. "In case you didn't notice, this institution is different from what you're probably used to. This is not the 'hood." The squirrely dude laughs, but Maverick shoots him a look. "We have a code here. The key word being *honor*. Honor above all else."

The squirrely dude stands at attention. "'A cadet will not lie, cheat, steal, nor tolerate those who do.'" He clears his throat. "'Mine honor is my life; both grow in one. Take honor from me, and my life is done.' Sir!"

"That's some good Shakespeare there," says Maverick. "See, we look at ourselves as the guardians of this code, and we'll bring honor to this school and to our good name at all costs. So, if you even *think* of disparaging our honor in any way, you'll be finding yourself on the wrong end of my stick."

"Your stick?" I ask.

"His *mallet*," says Big Red, pulling one out of the equipment wagon. "He's the best number two in the state. He wields a wicked stick, like true blue Cavalry."

I don't know if I'd be calling myself number two, I think.

He throws Maverick the mallet, and Maverick grabs it in midair and holds it like a rifle, standing at attention. I notice it's got a lightning bolt burned into it.

"This is my mallet!" Maverick yells. "There are many like it, but this one is mine! My mallet is my best friend! It is my life! I must master it as I must master my life!"

"You takin' this a little serious, don't ya think?" I say.

The other two grab mallets and line up behind him, holding them like rifles too as they do their routine. "Without me, my mallet is useless!" They shout in unison. "Without my mallet, *I* am useless! I must swing my mallet true! I must shoot straighter than my attacker, who is trying to beat me! I must score before he scores!"

I am starting to feel like I am in the wrong place. Even more than before.

They twirl their sticks around. "Before God I swear this creed: 'My mallet and myself are defenders of my team. We are the masters of my enemy; we are the saviors of the game! So be it, until there is only victory!' *Hooyah!*"

Whoa.

Maverick mounts his horse and trots toward me until he looms over me and presses the head of his mallet against my shoulder. His steel-blue eyes pierce mine. I can smell lunch on his breath.

"Just so you know, we're gonna ride you hard because we ride each other hard. We are all about excellence here, about representing this stable to the best of our ability at all costs. You down with that, *stable boy?*"

I hold my ground. "My name is Cole. But some people call me the Train, 'Cause if you get me goin', I'll run you down like a—" My mind goes blank.

"Like a *train?*" He bursts out laughing. That didn't come out quite the way I wanted it to.

"Well, *Train*, we should introduce ourselves if you're going to work for Charlie Company, or what we call C Troop." He rides back to join the others. "C stands for *cavalry*, as in *Here comes the cavalry to the rescue*. We are considered the best polo squad in the tri-state area. We play to win, which means we do *not* like to lose. We work hard, we play hard, and we study hard. I'm the squad leader on this team." I notice on the front of his helmet, it actually says Maverick.

Great. I'm working in a *Top Gun* schoolboy fantasy.

He kicks at his pony, who leaps into action. Maverick wields his mallet like a sword and whacks a ball lying on the dirt. I drop to the ground, and it goes sailing past me into the wood goal.

"Hooyah!"

"Welcome to the ring," he says, riding around me. "We play indoor arena polo. There're four chukkers in a match—that's like an inning or a quarter for you, but you knew that, right?" He laughs. "It's tighter in here and more physical than outdoor polo. It's all hooking and bumping—and we do like to mix it up."

I pick myself up off the dirt and try not to act bothered.

"There are three positions in arena polo. The number one position is the sprinter—our own fast and furious scorer, our frontline attack," he says. "Bandit!"

The squirrelly dude with a number 1 on his shirt jumps up onto his pony: "I'll hook your shot and rob you blind like a bandit. Next thing you know, it's in the goal."

I roll my eyes.

He yells *"Heyup!"* and goes from zero to sixty in a second and comes flying toward me. He taps at a ball, one-two-three, before whacking it around me into the goal. *Boom!* He trots back and high-fives Maverick.

"Number two is me, team captain," says Maverick. "I'm like the quarterback. I scan the field, call out the play, hit the long ball, or run interference. I always find my number one and set him up to score. I have to have the most field smarts to coordinate our plan of attack."

"MVP! MVP!" chants Big Red.

Maverick points at him. "Our number three there is our Back, the Brick Wall. He's the defender, the last man between the enemy and the goal."

Big Red mounts his ride, front and center. I notice that the number 3 on his jersey looks like it's made of bricks. "They call me Brick. They say big men are no good for polo, but I can block anything with my stick and kick it back upstream while you're sitting there with your thumb in your mouth. If you try riding up on me, you might as well be charging a brick wall. I'm going to stop you, one way or the other." He pounds his chest like a gorilla. I wouldn't wanna mess with him.

His pony takes a few steps and he smacks the ball so hard, it flies into the backstop and sticks into a crack in the wall. He nods like that could be my head. "Get that out for me, will ya, Train?"

They gather in the middle and face me down like they on a recruiting poster for the Marines. "Together, we're the George Washington Academy Generals," says Maverick. Then he adds, like he's reading poetry out loud: "'Associate with men of good quality if you esteem your own reputation; for it is better to be alone than in bad company.'"

"Huzzah!" they all shout in unison.

I try not to act too impressed. "Let me guess . . . Shakespeare said that, right?"

Maverick shakes his head. "No, Train. That's George Washington, our school's namesake. But don't worry, you'll get there. For now, why don't you get those balls for us, will ya?"

I swallow my pride and grab the balls and throw them back out. I'm about to pick out the one stuck in the wall when I hear them shout *"Heyup!"* I can feel the ground rumble as the Three Horsemen of the Apocalypse come charging toward me in line, moving the ball back and forth between them.

I'm standing there like a idiot when I realize they're not gonna go around me. So right when Maverick winds up, I hit the dirt and cover my head.

Thwack! I can feel the wind of the ball as it sails about a foot above me and smacks into the goal. But they keep coming, and suddenly the pounding of the hoofs surrounds me. Even with my eyes shut tight, I can feel the horses kicking up dirt and hear the riders laughing and yelling and singing some kind of military charging song as they mix it up. It seems to go on forever, until I hear a girl's voice sound off:

"Hey! Leave him alone!"

Someone—Brick, I think—says, "Look out, boys.

We have awakened the freak."

Bandit pipes up: "Don't get too close—she might rub off on you!"

I can hear a pony galloping closer and closer, and then the boys disperse, laughing, catcalling and exchanging insults. I hear *Acid Face*, *Spots*, and *Checkerboard*.

My heart is racing; I try to catch my breath. The pony slows down and stops in front of me. It flaps its lips, and I feel its spittle on me as it nudges me from overhead.

"Guess scrimmaging is not like you thought it'd be, huh?" says the voice.

I open one eye and see the horse's nostrils in my face. Then my eye changes focus, and I see it's the girl with the black-and-white skin staring down at me. And she's wearing one of *their* polo shirts.

What the . . . ?

I look away from her face. "What are you doin' here?" I ask.

"I should ask you the same. You following me?"

"No."

She stares at me, deciding if I am friend or foe. "You should probably get up. Don't want Ms. Whitman thinking you're lying down on the job."

"Funny." I sit up and shake the dirt out of my hair and face. "Nice friends you got there."

She looks over at the boys at the other end of the arena. "I wouldn't call them my friends."

I glance up at her face, and I can't help but stare. It still looks like she's wearing some kinda weird black-and-white makeup, but I know it's real. When she catches me staring, I lower my eyes to her polo uniform instead. "You go to school here?"

She don't seem too happy about it. "My mom's idea. On account of they have a horse program."

I get up on one knee, then stand and brush off my jeans. "I didn't know girls went here."

"They don't, technically," she says. "I'm part of the 'Great Experiment.'"

"What's that?"

She sighs like she's tired of explaining. "I'm the first girl at Washington Academy. First black kid in C Troop. First freak on the polo squad. But I'm just a day student. They don't have any boarding quarters for girls."

I watch the boys messing around, seeing who's the most macho of the group. "How'd they come to pick you?" I ask.

"My mom threatened to sue them if they didn't change their bylaws."

I laugh. "I guess you must be pretty popular around here, then."

"If you mean being called Spots or Acid Face every day and never getting a chance to play, or being given the worst pony in the stable, then, yeah, I guess I'm a lock for Homecoming Queen."

"You got a *Top Gun* name too?" I ask.

She looks at me funny, then gets it. "I don't use the name they gave me. You can call me Ruthie. This is my pony, Patches."

Patches is spotty, just like her. I wonder if that was the joke when they gave him to her, but I don't say anything. "I'm Cole."

I hear a *thwack*, and a ball rolls up toward her. A challenge. She glances down at the ball, then back at me. "First thing you need to know is they see everything as a battle, not a game. It's all or nothing. You play to win or go home," she says. She glares at them, steels herself.

"Duty calls." She clicks her tongue and springs into action, moving down the court.

I notice her jersey number is 0.

Tap-tap-tap. She takes the ball toward them, galloping downfield as the boys break ranks and come at her from all sides. She looks good, fearless. The goal looms at the other end, but right when she gets a good bead on it, Maverick rides up on her and pushes her into Brick, who hooks her mallet with his, causing her to miss the ball.

Next thing I know, she's halfway off her horse, one foot dragging on the dirt, and the boys clear out. Bandit scoops the ball up with his mallet, tipping it over to Maverick, who palms it and rides it back to Ruthie.

She's barely holding on to the saddle, her boot caught in her stirrup, unable to get up or down. Maverick drops the ball by her side. "Nice try, Spots. It's good to dream—but not against the Dream Team, girl. You know the drill. You just earned muck-raking duties today!"

They laugh, and she glances over at me with a look I'm getting to know well. Something tells me we're gonna be in this together, whether we like it or not.

EIGHT

I'm beat. It feels like the longest day of my life: working the Ritz before dawn, first day of school, then a good hazing at the military academy. My body aches, my head hurts, and I'm tired as hell. Worse yet, I gotta take the bus home, which drops me a good ten blocks away. Good thing I got no homework to do.

After the bus, I'm walking through Strawberry Mansion in a daze when I hear, "Yo, cuz. Yo!" I look over and see Smush at the wheel of a new ride. He pulls up and stops as I check out his car.

He looks . . . different. New haircut, gold chain and bracelet, dope threads. And now he has wheels? "When'd you start drivin'?" I ask.

"Like my new chariot? I call her Sharanda. Hop in—I'll give you a ride."

I get in, wincing as I shut the door.

"Man, you look like you been put through the wringer today," he says.

"Yeah, just about. Started school at North and got a job."

He looks at me like I'm crazy. "You got a job, cuz? What the hell for?"

"Harp said if I wanted to stay in Philly, I gotta pay my way. He even lined up the job for me. At the military academy."

That sets him off. He starts laughing, then totally loses it. "Damn, that Harp is one tough mofo. Good thing he your daddy, or no tellin' what he'd do to you. He ain't even speakin' to me right now."

That's news to me. "Why? You're his sister's only son."

"Yeah, well, he got too many rules. Sometimes I wish he would clear outta my life like my moms and pops did. Leave me alone. He definitely don't like my new line of business."

I know one thing about Smush. When he say 'business,' I know it probably ain't legal. He's a true hustler. In fact, I notice he ain't driving straight back to Chester Ave. "You don't mind if we make a quick stop, do ya?"

I shake my head. I'm too exhausted to walk. "Whatever."

He sighs. "Man, I hate to see you like this. No fourteen-year-old should be working. Ain't there laws against that?"

"It's off the books. It's more like I'm payin' off debts."

He whistles. "Dang, that Harp is cold. Got you workin' for him *good*. And school? You going to North?"

I nod. He can read my feelings about that place on my face. "That place is for suckers—no offense. That's why I quit. They just want to control you and take the spit outta you any way they can."

I ain't gonna argue.

We drive down toward Brewerytown, and you can see how the place is changing on a daily basis. New condos, new coffeehouses, craft brewery, yoga.

Smush sees it too. "Man, this place is goin' downhill." We come to a stop at a light and watch as some bearded white hipster crosses the street with a

Chihuahua in one of them baby pouches attached to his back. "Only thing it's good for is new customers."

"Customers?"

He pulls into a parking lot behind a Popeyes and kills the engine. "Hungry?" he asks.

My stomach growls in answer.

"Yeah, you ain't eaten all day, I see." He pulls out a wad—and I mean a wad—of cash and peels off two twenties. "Get whatever you want and times it by two for me."

I'm too hungry to ask questions, so I snatch the money before he changes his mind. I hustle in to get some eats, and just the smell revives me a bit.

When I come out with two big bags of food and drink, I see him talking to some shady-looking dude in a leather jacket and hoodie. They exchange something, and when the guy sees me coming, he moves on quickly.

"Who was that?" I ask when I get in the car again.

"Business. Whatchou got for me?" he asks, rubbing his hands together.

We lay out our feast and dive in. I almost swallow mine whole.

"Whoa there, cowboy. You do know about chewing, right? Don't Harp feed you?" he asks.

"No," I say, mouth full. "He makes me eat at school."

"Figures," he says, then slurps down half his Coke, watching me the whole time.

When I finish my last fry and my last sip of drink, I sit back like I just had Thanksgiving dinner. "Dang, that was good," I say, sleepy.

"Damn right, cuz. You should be eatin' like this every day."

"I wish. I ain't even bein' paid in cash."

He shakes his head. "Now, that's just wrong. A

man should always have something to show for his efforts." He reaches in and peels off a couple twenties. He pauses, then peels off a few more. "Here you go, youngblood. Somebody got to take care of you."

I look at the cash. I know Harp would not approve. "Nah, man. I'm good."

"Are you? A man needs to have cash for extracurricular activities, if you know what I mean. Any girls in your life?"

I shake my head. "Nah, man. Girls at school look at me like I'm a alien."

He studies me, looks at my clothes. "That's 'cause you dressin' like a cowboy. You in high school, you got to dress to impress, ya feel me? We should go shopping, do you a makeover. When's the last time you got your hair coiffed?"

I don't know what that is, but I know I ain't never had it done.

"Exactly. You need to take care of yourself, and then the ladies will notice. Me? I got two girls right now." He nudges me in the shoulder. I laugh it off.

"I ain't in no hurry. I'm only a freshman."

He laughs. "I'm just messin' with you, cuz. Take the paper anyways. A down payment."

"For what?" I ask.

He shrugs. "My operation is growin'. I could use some family in the organization. You could come in handy."

"What happened to Snapper?" I ask. "You two used to always be tight."

He goes silent, like I touched a nerve. "That dude betrayed me."

"How?"

He sighs. "Got a girl knocked up and all a sudden decides to get married and get a real job and all a that. Said he couldn't hang wit' me no more. Can you believe that?"

"It happens," I say, but still I know Harp would definitely not approve of me working for Smush.

"Me, I'm thinkin' ahead. Makin' some green, puttin' it aside for a rainy day. You should too." He presses the cash into my hand, and I don't give it back.

He starts the car and we drive on. By the time we get back to the neighborhood, I am fast asleep.

NINE

I wake up with a start. I don't know where I am until my eyes adjust to the darkness.

My room. I lay my head back down. I don't remember going to bed, but here I am . . . still in the clothes I wore today?

My eyes wander over to the stairs, and I see a dark red spot growing brighter. It's Harp, sitting on the stairs, smoking and staring off into the darkness.

"What time is it?" I ask.

"Late. The question is, Do *you* know what time it is?"

I can hear music turned real low. Coltrane. I don't know much jazz, but my namesake, him I know. Harp made sure of that. And one thing I know, when Coltrane is on, Harp's mind is wandering into dark places.

There's a long pause, and I can feel him staring at me, even though I can't see his eyes.

"I want you to have a future, Cole," he finally says.

"Me too," I say. *Why wouldn't I?*

"You know we got to work twice as hard, bow twice as low, and hold our heads up twice as high to get ahead. I don't want you to make the same mistakes I did."

He shifts, takes a deep drag. "I don't want you to end up like Smush."

Now I know where this is going. He musta seen Smush drop me off. "He was just givin' me a ride. He all right."

I hear him get up and walk to the bottom of the stairs. His face comes into view, lit up by the streetlight coming through the window. "There's three paths for a young black brother like you in Strawberry Mansion. One takes you to prison, the second to the cemetery. The only one worthwhile involves college and getting out of here."

"What's wrong with here? I thought horses have been good for us. Good for the community."

"For now. But that isn't going to give you a future. North isn't going to give you a future."

"It's what I got."

He walks up to me, drops money onto my chest. "Found this in your pockets. *That* will definitely not get you a future. It'll get you dead. If I can do one thing for you, it's steer you clear of the likes of Smush, you hear?"

I sigh. "But he's family."

He pokes me in the chest till it hurts. "He's the wrong kind of family. Just stay clear. Got it?" I can see in his eyes he means it.

"I got it," I say.

"Good. Now go back to sleep."

He turns and trudges upstairs, his feet dragging across the wood floor above. *Go back to sleep?* Yeah, right. I stare at the ceiling and listen to him pacing for a good hour.

TEN

The Academy tack room is where they keep all their polo equipment and horse gear. Saddles, halters, and bridles, all oiled and cleaned, hang on the wall, thanks to me. Mallets, helmets, and leather armor sit in the equipment wagon, waiting to be sorted. I'm folding blankets and cleaning bits when I look over and see Ruthie watching me.

"You been quiet all day."

"Are you followin' me?" I give her a slight smile so she knows I'm joking, but turn away 'cause I don't want her to catch me staring at her face.

There's a awkward pause, but then she says, "You wish." She walks in and grabs a hoof-pick and comb. But she just kinda stands there, watching me.

"So, what's it like?" she asks. "You know, being a cowboy."

"It's not like here, I'll tell you that."

"Meaning?"

"Meanin' . . ." I look around, and my eyes land on some saddles. "Like those saddles. You guys use them weird little saddles—"

"They're called English."

"Exactly," I say. "English-style riding. English is all about the rules. We ride Western, which is about bein' free. English-style means standing on stirrups to ride, like a jockey. Western, we ride like the Old West—free."

"In the city?" she asks.

"Yeah, in the city. And we race too. At the Speedway. Way faster than anybody here."

"At the racetracks?"

I give her a look. "No. At the park. Fairmount Park? Don't you guys trail-ride there?"

"Sometimes. But we have to get special permission or be in an official event."

She proves my point. "Exactly."

I start sorting through the helmets and putting them away in cubbyholes, but she still standing there. "Maybe you could show me sometime."

"What, the Speedway?" I say, surprised.

"Yeah, or your barn. I never rode in the streets before. I'd have to use one of your ponies, though," she says.

"What about Patches?"

"Against the rules to take the ponies off campus," she says. "Anyone who boards here isn't allowed off campus unless they have weekend leave. But since I don't board here, I'm free after school. Maybe you'll let me ride Boo, like old times."

"Old times?" I ask.

"Yeah, I used to ride Boo before I got Patches."

Wait a sec. "So, you *did* ride Boo before."

Ruthie nods. "Of course. Who do you think taught him how to be a polo pony?"

I blink. "A what?"

She smiles. "He was a good student too."

I'm having a hard enough time picturing Boo under someone else's care. I can't imagine him going up against them cadets and their ponies.

"How'd he do?" I ask, not sure if I really wanna know.

"He's a natural," Ruthie says. "At first, he was scared of the mallet and the ball, but I just started carrying it around as we rode, then started swinging it slowly around him till he got used to it. But the ball freaked him out, so I ended up putting a few balls in his water trough until he got used to seeing them too. Then he actually started playing fetch with me. I'd hit the ball, and he'd go chase it down."

I gotta admit, it kinda bothers me that Boo would betray me and play with someone else. But then I remember I was the one who left him behind.

"Did he go up against them other guys—the Generals?"

"Sometimes. But I kept him safe—don't worry. He held his own. I was about to take him to the next level when I guess you came back and reclaimed him."

"Well, he *is* my horse," I say.

She nods. "I can tell. Now *you* just need to learn how to play polo."

I look up at her. "I ain't no polo player. I'm a cowboy."

Ruthie winks. "Don't knock it till you try it. I could teach you. Like I taught Boo."

I let that sink in. But something makes me say, "Boo didn't have a say in the matter. Cowboys don't polo. No offense, but we just don't go in for that sissy stuff."

Now she gives me the full-on evil eye. "I know you just didn't call the most dangerous sport in the world 'sissy stuff.' If you aren't man enough, just say so."

"You call this dangerous? I play b-ball down at the courts on Diamond Drive. You can get shot there."

She sighs. "Look, polo is crazy intense. You're trying to hit a tiny moving ball from a moving horse that weighs a thousand pounds, charging at forty miles per hour. Your head is eight feet off the ground, and your mallet is over four feet long, and you're trying to aim at a ball as big as a baseball while you're leaning halfway off, trying to punch it into a goal without being trampled to death as you're being rushed by three other players, also on thousand-pound beasts, waving hammers at you!"

I hold up my hand like I didn't mean nothing by it. "I'm just sayin' it ain't my game. I cowboy and play b-ball. Besides, too many white people play polo."

I can feel her eyes bore into my head. "Do I look white to you?" she says.

It's a trick question. Girls always be doing that to you. *Do I look fat in this dress?* You doomed either way. But this is even trickier, 'cause from certain angles, she do look white, or at least like she *becoming* white.

I can tell I'm taking too long to answer. "No," I say weakly. "But you the only sister out here that I can see."

Ruthie nods. "Maybe that's why I could use a *brother* in my corner."

She got me there.

"Or maybe you're too embarrassed to be seen with me, like all the others?" she asks.

"I didn't say that."

She crosses her arms. "So, then . . . you must be chicken?"

She had to say it.

Next thing I know, Ruthie got me up on her pony, Patches, in the middle of the arena, with a mallet in my hand. The saddle is all weird, and the stirrups are way too high for me.

"Uh, you got any normal saddles?" I ask.

"We ride with the stirrups high like a jockey, remember? That's how you stand up to maneuver a strike."

"We don't stand in our stirrups," I say. "Only thing we stand up on is our saddles, when we showin' off." Even on Patches I can do it, so I show her. She's not impressed, so I sit back down.

"Normally, it might take two or three months to turn a basic rider into a polo player," she says. "But since you're already a good rider, you should be able to handle the moves quicker."

"When I race, I can do fifty on Boo at the Speedway. I can roll back and jump over two hay squares too."

She smiles, like she might to a Little Leaguer bragging that he can play in the majors. "That's good. Now take that mallet, rotate your body, and just swing it back and forth, like a pendulum on a clock."

"What's a pendulum?" I ask.

Ruthie rolls her eyes. "Just swing it back and forth, like you're brushing the sand."

"Why didn't you just say that?"

I do it. Easy. She has me doing this for a good five minutes on either side of the horse till I think it's a joke. "How about addin' a ball?"

She throws a ball down. "Think you can hit that?"

"Seriously? Watch and learn," I say.

Swing—miss.

Swing—miss.

Swing. I graze it, and it rolls about a foot.

"Nice," she says. "You know when I said Boo was a natural?"

Now she's the smart-ass.

"That's 'cause I gotta be movin'," I say. I nudge Patches and we gallop out a few yards, then turn back around. "Check this out."

Charge. *Swing.* I knock the ball sideways and almost nail Patches in the head with the mallet, sending him dancing in circles till I drop the mallet to get control back with two hands.

She shakes her head, then grabs the mallet, walks over, and holds her hand out.

"What?"

She looks annoyed. "Help me up?"

Horses aren't made for two, but whatever. I take her hand, help swing her up behind me—a little too close if you ask me. I can suddenly feel her body heat on my back, her breath on my neck. "Take the mallet," she says.

I do. Our hands brush, and I feel a weird sensation in my gut. "Pretend the mallet is an extension of your hand. You ever play handball?"

"*Please.* I grew up in the streets. If we weren't playin' basketball, we was playin' handball in the park," I say.

"Okay, then. Do like that. Swipe like you're going to hit the ball clean."

She places one hand on my back, to straighten and

rotate my posture, then puts her other hand on mine and brings back my arm high, ready to strike.

I'm feeling all right until—

"Well, ain't that a picture. Spots and the cowboy sure are getting close."

Brick. Just what I needed.

My gut instinct is to deny anything is going on, but I remember what she said about being embarrassed to be seen with her.

"Is he your new boyfriend?" asks Bandit behind him.

Great, more than one.

"I dunno. Is Brick yours?" she asks. Good one.

Brick blanches at the thought. "Shouldn't you be working, stable boy?"

Suddenly, I got no good comebacks. My mind goes blank.

Ruthie keeps going. "I was just showing him a thing or two. Turns out, he's faster than any of you," she adds. "Even Bandit."

This just keeps getting better. Now Bandit moseys up to us. "On horse or just running away?" he says.

"Maybe you should race him and find out," she adds.

"Maybe you don't wanna make challenges for me," I whisper.

"Oh, look at that. Whispering in her ear," says Brick. "How cute. Freaks in love."

That's it. I pull the reins over and canter straight to them.

"Easy, Cole," she says, holding on to me.

"I got this," I say. They're on foot, so being on horse means instant respect. I get up right in their faces. They look a little unnerved but hold their ground.

"You were sayin'?" I ask.

Brick is thinking about his options. I hope one of them isn't tackling Patches.

"So, what—you think you're a polo player now?" he asks. "Maybe you wanna jump into the ring with us and show us what you got?"

I know that's a sucker bet. "What, you afraid to race?" I counter.

"Enough!"

It's Coach Whitman, walking in from the sidelines. I shoot Brick a look. "Lucky for you . . ."

She sizes up the situation. "Cole, I need you to attend to the tack room. Ruthie, I thought you were prepping for the commander's parade review this afternoon. In fact, I thought you all were supposed to prep. Do you have your dress uniforms?"

"Yes, ma'am," they all answer.

"Good, then get to it." She waits for us to disperse.

As they head to the barn, Ruthie pulls me aside and says, "I need you in my corner. I'll train you, and we'll show those boneheads what's what."

She heads to the back, and I go to the tack room, unsure where all this is headed. Last thing I need is to get in the middle of a fight that ain't my own. I mean, I was happy to stand up to protect the stables last year. That became my fight. But I ain't going down over *polo*.

ELEVEN

The parade turns out to be a all-hands-on-deck review march, in full regalia, in front of the commander and his top brass from the school and a nearby military base. Coach asks me to stay till after the parade so I can help stable the horses.

I walk over and sit on the far end of the bleachers as about three hundred cadets in their crazy best uniforms (black with red stripes, gold shoulder things, some with medals) march past a stand where the commander and his staff stand and proudly salute the procession. Turns out, he's a actual commander, retired, and running the Academy. With him are a buncha older army and marine types, also dressed in their finest. The cadets march in unison in perfect rows with the band leading the way. Bringing up the rear is C Troop: the cavalry.

The four of them, Maverick, Brick, Bandit, and Ruthie, are dressed in a different version of their usual uniforms. They're wearing dark-blue cavalry hats too, like the kind Custer wore in that movie we saw at school. They all have swords at their sides, which is badass, though Maverick's is the biggest. I gotta admit, seeing them and their ponies marching as they take out their swords and salute the commander with them is pretty awesome. Their ponies don't even flinch when the cannons are fired off. But Ruthie—she stands out like a sore thumb. Everyone looks so perfect, but she the only girl, and her face—well, nobody else look like her, that's for sure.

But what gets me is when I see some of the grown-ups pointing at her and whispering to each other, even laughing. They're as bad as the kids! I get so pissed off, I leave the bleachers before I say something stupid. The last thing I want is to get Ruthie in trouble.

I sit in the barn and wait for them to file in. I feel—I don't know—mad, confused, embarrassed for her. Maybe everyone feels like a freak in high school. But if people see you as a *actual* freak—that's messed up.

When they come in, the boys stable their ponies and put away their gear. I hear them making fun of Ruthie behind her back, saying she's the "special needs kid we use to raise money," and stuff like that. I stay quiet, not sure what I wanna say to her. She is the last one in, so I go to help her put away her gear. She seem a little down.

"Why you even do this?" I ask. "All a this—it ain't normal."

She tries joking her way out. "Maybe you haven't noticed, but—"

"Don't say that." But I have a hard time looking her in the face, and I hate myself for feeling that way. "I mean, I know you love ponies and polo, but to put up with all this . . . Why you even wanna be a part of a group that don't want you?"

She dumps her saddle onto a crate in the tack room. "My mom says being a leader means setting an example. And being an example means you gotta stand out. Standing *out* means standing *up* to something. You should understand that."

"Why me?" I ask.

"Because I know who you are. You're that kid from Chester Ave. who stood up to the City. I saw you on TV."

She remembers that? "Yeah, but . . . that felt good. I wasn't doin' that for attention, but for our way of life."

She's facing away from me, but I see her catching her reflection in a small, dirty mirror hanging on the wall. "Maybe I don't want to hide anymore. Maybe if I'm wearing a uniform or competing in a polo match, people will be looking at me for that and not because—not because. And besides, if I can stick to it and graduate from here, I'll go to college on a polo scholarship."

I believe her, even if I don't think she quite believes herself. "You better than them, ya know," I say.

She looks at me in the mirror. "You think so?"

"I know so. You should come to my world. People down there will look at you for what you are."

"And what is that?" she asks, sounding mad.

I don't have to think about that. "Ruthie. Who likes ponies. And wants to go to college."

She looks at her reflection in the mirror for the longest time. I think maybe I should leave her be and am about to sneak out when she says, "Look at my face."

I stop. "What?"

She turns to me. "Look. At. My. Face."

I find myself staring at my feet. I can feel her frowning.

"Am I that ugly to you?" she asks, hurt.

Feet. Dirt. Ground. I mutter, "Um . . . no. It's just . . . it's just . . ."

"What?"

"I don't wanna be rude," I say, glancing up at her. Now she's staring me down. "You're being rude when you don't look in me in the eye."

I sigh. "But . . . people is always starin' at you, like, all the time." I think about the parade.

"So?"

"I don't wanna be like everyone else."

There's a long pause. "They might be looking, but they aren't seeing. I want you to *see*."

I nod, bring my eyes back up, and look into her eyes, staring hard. She returns my gaze, like she's searching for something.

"Now you're looking at my eyes, not my face," she says.

I blink. I know what she wants. So I step back half a step and refocus. I look at her face. But not like before. Like really . . . looking.

"What do you see?" she asks.

I see . . . her skin. How can you not? But I don't turn away. I force myself to really look at it. See *her*.

I try and look past the fact that she looks like someone threw paint or acid on her face. I focus on her skin. And I notice . . . it's smooth. No pimples or nothing. Her skin is dark and deep on the parts that are black. I notice the spots around her eyes, like someone dripped paint while she was sleeping. Around her mouth, the side of her nose, her chin . . . it's white. But really, it's whiter than white. White people got pink or tan skin. But hers is like . . . like she peeled off a layer and revealed the ivory-white underneath.

She even got white on a bit of her eyebrows and hair, right up over her right eye.

Her lips is full and glossy, with little white splotches near the left corner. Her nose is thick and flat, and I let my eyes wander up to hers and I see . . . hurt. Or maybe it's frustration. But then, when she sees me seeing her, her face relaxes.

"I see you," I say.

She almost smiles. Her eyes are soft, but not like she gonna cry.

"I see you too," she says, and suddenly I realize she been checking me out all this time. She reaches out, touches her finger to a spot right on my cheek. "Where'd you get that scar?"

I reach up to touch it, and she pulls her hand back. "That? Mama told me I got that when I was a baby and Harp put me up on a old horse called Chuck. I guess he bucked a little, and my head hit the front of the saddle and caught a buckle on the bridle or something before Harp pulled me off."

She looks at another spot on my face—a small cut I got on my left eyebrow. "And that?"

"Fight. Sixth grade. I lost."

She nods. I wanna ask her what it's like being . . . her. So I spit out, "You always had skin like that?"

Now *she's* the one looking down at her feet. Maybe I shouldn't have asked that. But she's the one that started this.

"Am *I* that ugly?" I say.

She holds back a comment and looks back up.

"So?" I ask.

She takes a deep breath, lets it out. "It started about five years ago, when I was nine." She feels her scalp, pushes aside her hair. "Mom noticed a white spot on my scalp. She was braiding my hair and says, "Oh! You musta been out in the sun too long or something. You got a white spot up here."

"Where'd it come from?" I ask.

She shrugs. "Don't know. Just happened. Next time she was doing my rows, I asked her if the spot was gone, but she didn't say nothing. Later, I looked in a mirror and I could see the spot had grown. A lot."

"Dang."

She nods. "By the time I was eleven, I had spots on my hands and around my eyes. My mom took me to the doctor, and that's when I heard the word *vitiligo* for the first time. Michael Jackson disease."

She's holding out her hands like she's showing me, and I suddenly find myself taking them in mine and looking at them closely.

"I like your hands," I say softly. I can feel her almost pull back, but she stops herself.

"Every year, it got worse," she say. "I stopped going out 'cause people would just stare. Then Mom took me outta school 'cause . . . just 'cause. You know how kids is."

"Yeah, I know."

"She homeschooled me, and when I went out, she put makeup on me. I wore gloves sometimes and hats and stuff. People stared even more wherever I went, like I was a burn victim or something." She laughs. "Little kids and old people were the worst. But at least little kids ask you straight up: 'What happened to your face?'"

I can't help but wonder . . . "But you ain't wearin' no makeup now."

"I got tired of hiding. One day, Mom took me out for ice cream—and I refused to wear makeup or hats anymore. "They're going to look at me one way or the other. Might as well give 'em something to look at."

"What'd she say?"

"She said she realized she had been shaming me by trying to make me something I'm not. That I was beautiful in my own way."

She does air quotes when she says "beautiful" and rolls her eyes.

"So why did you end up here?" I ask.

"I liked horses from when I was little, so Mom took me riding over in Bucks County. When we were there, we saw something going on in a big green field. They had white tents, and everyone was dressed in white too, drinking champagne and stuff. And then these ponies came out—polo ponies. We watched them play all afternoon."

"You were hooked?" I ask.

She nods. "My mom told me: 'Imagine you out there with all these people looking on. Wouldn't that be amazing?' I found out some of the players were from the Academy, and the next thing I knew, I was looking into it online. I showed Mom, and she found a way to make it happen."

"I get it," I say. "I guess you gotta do what you gotta do."

"You can hide and be ashamed of your skin, or you can stand up and show 'em you aren't afraid. Be an example." Ruthie smiles. Exhales. Eyes on me.

And for the first time I notice, she actually is kinda beautiful.

TWELVE

On the way to the bus stop, I find myself floating. I feel all warm inside—until I turn the corner and see Smush sitting in his car.

"Finally! I been waitin' for your butt a half hour, cuz," he says, starting the car.

I walk over. "If Harp sees you drivin' me home, he's gonna whup my butt or ground me. Maybe both."

He's looking at me funny. "What's up with you? You look all dreamy-eyed or something."

I blush but shake it off. "Nothin'. Nothin's up."

He smiles, but I can tell he don't believe me. "Whatever, cuz. Get in. Harp won't see us. I just need a favor." He pops the lock on the door.

"That's what I'm afraid of." I get in. "What's up?"

Smush adjusts his rearview mirror like he's on the lookout. "Bruh, we family, right?"

I sigh. "I guess."

"Okay, then. I just need you to do one little thing, cuz . . ." When someone says they need a little favor, it's never little. But I don't say no. We drive a bit and wind up in a empty parking lot in a neighborhood I don't know.

"Where are we?" I ask.

"Where we need to be, cuz. Stop askin' questions. See that car over there?"

"The tricked-out one with the gold rims?"

"Yeah. Take this package over there. Give it to the dude in the driver seat, and he'll give you something back."

"Why don't *you* do it?"

He acts all offended. "I'm tryin' to throw you some scraps, young buck. I'm a businessman, and it don't look good if I'm actin' as delivery boy too. Just do me a solid, and there'll be a good tip in it for you, ya feel me?"

"A tip?"

"For a minute of work? I don't think you in a position to say no, cuz. Or maybe you got *too* much money in your pocket?"

I sigh. "Fine. Give it to me."

He reaches in back and hands me a oversize brown envelope. "What is this?" I ask.

He throws up his hands. "Ain't you never seen a movie? Don't you know the mule never asks questions or they get whacked?"

In my heart, I know I shouldn't do this, but Smush is my cousin. And the money sounds good too. "Whatever."

I get out and look around to see if there are any cops. This don't feel legal, but it seems simple enough.

I start walking toward the car. I can't see the guy in there too good 'cause the sun shining on his windshield. But when I get to the driver side, I stop cold. Dude looks hard-core, like he means business. His tats, all guns and dollar signs, send a chill down the back of my neck.

Then I hear a click. I look back and see another guy, pointing a gun at Smush! Smush is getting outta his car as the guy puts the barrel to his head.

I can't believe what I'm seeing.

"Hey," says a voice.

I turn back to the guy in the car. "I think that's mine." He reaches out and snatches the package from my hand. "I hear Smush been dealin' in my territory. Where I come from, that's bad business. And that's too bad for you—"

"RUN!"

I whip around just in time to see Smush knock the other dude down and take off down the street. And suddenly, I'm like Usain Bolt running the hundred-yard dash. I don't even look back to see if the guy in the car is pulling out a gun—I'm gone. Around a corner, down a alley. I try to pretend I'm Boo at the Speedway, riding the straightaway.

Then I hear the car coming up on us fast. We hit a fence and scramble up over it, scratching the hell outta my legs.

Now I'm running for my life. "You set me up!" I shout at Smush. He's running two steps ahead of me like he's used to this. Me? Not so much.

I'm gonna strangle Smush when I catch up to him. But only if they don't catch us first.

We hop another fence, run down some stairs, jump a gate, and move along a cement wall till we find an escape: a ladder leading down into a abandoned subway station. We climb down and hide in the dark, listening for footsteps.

"I think . . . we lost 'em," Smush says, out of breath.

I listen. Nothing but the sound of my heart beating out my chest.

Then I hit him as hard as I can in the arm.

"OW! Dang, cuz, what's that for?"

I give him a look: *Seriously?*

He sighs. "How was I supposed to know? I didn't mean for it to go down like this. I'd never put you in harm's way. Honest." When people say "honest," they basically lying.

I hit him again. "But you did!"

"Stop it!" he says.

We hear a kicked bottle skitter across the cement. "*Shh!* Come on." He heads into the tunnel. I follow.

I make a promise to myself: *Just let me get out of this alive, and I'll do as Harp says.*

When we finally emerge out a sewer grate, it's dark. I decide I'm gonna walk the rest of the way.

"Come on, cuz, don't be like that!" he begs. "I'll take you shoppin' for some new threads like I promised. You'll forget all about this when you lookin' fine for the ladies!"

But I've had it. Two hours ago, I was feeling great. Now I feel lucky not to have a bullet in my back.

I hear him cussing himself out, but I don't care. I'm gone.

THIRTEEN

When I get home, I think about telling Harp everything, but he's not in a good mood, so I just pretend like I was working late. He grunts, and I go to my room. But I can't sit still; my mind is still racing. I gotta tell someone about today, but who?

I take out my phone and punch in a number I know by heart.

"Hello?"

I take a deep breath. "It's me, Mama."

There's a long pause. "What's going on, baby?" she says softly.

I realize I can't tell her about what just went down without freaking her out, so I don't know why I called her. I just did. "You know, just keepin' on."

She knows me. "Not as easy as you thought?" She ain't gloating.

"Maybe. A lot goin' on."

"Like?"

"Like . . . Harp got me a job."

I know she can't imagine me working. "So, you're a working man now."

"And school sucks."

"Hmm . . ."

"And I don't even got time for Boo. I'm up at dawn and don't get back till dark. I can't keep up with homework, and Smush is gettin' into all kind of things he shouldn't . . ."

"Sounds like a lot."

There's a long pause.

"Maybe . . . I shoulda gone back with you."

I'm waiting for the *I told you so* . . . but instead she says, "No. I think it's good."

What? "How's this good?" I ask.

99

"Sometimes we have to go through the fire to figure out what we really want."

What do I want? "I guess there's no chance we could all be a family again?" I know that's not fair to say, but I say it anyways.

She sighs. "We never were a family, baby. You can't get back what never was."

We sit and listen to the sound of us breathing.

"And then there's . . . this girl," I add.

I can feel her eyebrows raise from here. "A girl? What's she like?"

"She's a horse person."

She laughs. "That's good, I guess."

"But she plays . . . polo."

"Polo? Like, on a horse polo?" she asks.

"Yeah."

Long pause.

"Is she white?"

I'm not sure how to answer that. "Not really?"

"What?"

How do I say this? "She's . . . kinda becomin' white, I guess? But against her will."

"That makes no sense, Cole."

"She got that Michael Jackson disease," I say.

She wasn't expecting that. "Oh."

"She looks . . . different."

"Okay . . . and does that embarrass you?" she asks.

"I don't know. Maybe. 'Cause they make fun of her. And me."

"Who's they?" she asks.

I don't really wanna get into it. "Just bullies, I guess."

"And what are you gonna do about it?"

What am *I gonna do about it?* I think. "I haven't thought that far."

"Hmm . . ." she says.

"So, what about you? Are you . . . lonely?" I wanna hear her say *yes*.

There's another pause. "I've been exploring my options."

Options? I don't wanna hear about her dating.

"I been looking at other jobs," she says. "Honestly, I need a change. I don't like coming home and not seeing you on my couch."

"The couch was not that good, Mama. At least I got my own room here. Sort of." I think of the former horse stall I'm sleeping in.

Then she hits me with this: "I've been thinking about moving."

That takes me by surprise. "But . . . you've been there forever."

She pauses. "Forever is never forever. People grow up, get older, move on . . ."

I guess so . . .

"Who knows?" she adds. "Maybe I'll move back to Philly."

That one leaves me speechless.

FOURTEEN

Soon, I get stuck in a daily routine where every day is the same as the next, and I start losing track of time.

Dawn with Boo. *Feed, muck, groom.* If I get up early enough, I go for a short ride around the vacant lot.

School, where I go from one class to the next. I don't know why, but I don't seem to make friends. I thought my fame with the uprising woulda made me a guy with a rep, but around here, something that happened more than a year ago might as well be ancient history. I even try to bring it up in social studies, but my teacher pins me as a troublemaker.

One day, as a joke, Harp hides my kicks and I have to wear them stupid cowboy boots he gave me, the ones he wore as a kid. Even the new security guard looks at me funny.

"You gonna wear those in *there?*" he asks at the metal detector. I shrug, not wanting to get into it.

After that, I earn the nickname *Country*.

Now everyone looks at me as some kinda hick. The bangers won't stop hassling me, and one day, they corner me in the bathroom, looking to send a message.

That's when I learn cowboy boots is good for one thing: kicking.

I get all Bruce Lee on them fools, but all I get is the principal's office, a black eye, and a cut lip.

Principal Butler is a big black woman who dresses African style and carries a bullhorn. She is known for greeting everyone in the hallways by saying, "If nobody tells you they love you today, I love you. Now get your behind to class." She is a woman on a mission to make this school better.

Today, she in no mood. The other dudes are in the vice principal's office, and she is looking at my grades online, which aren't good.

"What are we gonna do with you, Cole?" she asks.

"How you mean?"

She looks at me long and hard, like she trying to figure me out. "Do you know I went to school with your daddy?"

No, I didn't. And I don't wanna hear if they was a thing. "No. I thought maybe you was from Kenya or someplace else."

"Just because I like to wear African print dresses or dashikis doesn't mean I come from the motherland—not more than we all do, if you go back far enough. Me, I was born and raised in Columbus, Ohio. Moved here when I was a teen, so I know a thing or two about being the new kid." She laughs. "Your dad was the first one to talk to me when I moved here. He didn't do too well in class, but he was one of the smartest guys I knew." I raise my eyebrows like *Really? We talking about the same guy?*

Now she gets up and says, "Follow me."

We walking down a empty hallway. On either side are classrooms. Some doors are open a crack, and you can peek in. Others are shut tight.

We stop in the middle of the hall, and she turns to me. "Someone once said this to me, so I'm saying it to you. Look around this hallway."

I do. It's the same kind of school hallway you see

anywhere. Lockers. Doors. Trash on the floor. Security cameras.

"Life is like this hallway," she says, pointing to one end, where there's a set of double doors. "You enter on one side. And then you start walking down the path of life." She looks me in the eye, considers her words. "We walk our path, either because we're told that's our path, or because we're just going along with everyone else." She then points to the other end, where there's a locked door with a EXIT sign over it. "We go through life, doing our thing, staying on the path until we die, then we exit to the great beyond."

This is getting dark, and I have no idea why she telling me this. "There are all kinds of obstacles in between, Cole. Hurdles, blocks, hoops you have to jump through or over. No skills, no job, bad company, gangs, prison. And worse."

Now I know where this is going.

"Don't roll your eyes, Cole. There's another point I'm making. You know as well as I do, just being a young black man from Strawberry Mansion makes your path. Sorry, that's just the way it is." She leans in close and looks me in the eye. "My job is to keep my young men alive and in the educational system, and if I'm lucky, *real* lucky, something inspires them or sparks something in them to take another path."

"What do you mean, 'another path'?" I ask.

She points to some of the open doors. "We pass all kinds of opportunities in life, and we don't even know it. We don't recognize them because we are told we are one thing and that's all we'll ever be. But if you're curious, like I was, you pass a door in the hallway of life and you see something going on inside that grabs your attention. Maybe you'll step off your path and onto a new one."

I can't tell if she's deep or full of it. She knows what I'm thinking, and she kind of laughs and shakes her head.

"I moved away from Philadelphia after high school. Got a PhD in education. I have traveled the world. I've even written a book, and I go around giving talks."

"Why you here, then?" I ask.

She smiles. "I'm here because everyone deserves a chance, and I'm trying to make a difference. I know this place has a long way to go. But I see something in this community worth investing in. And I see something in you too."

"Yeah? And what's that?"

She puts her hand on my shoulder. "A refusal to give in."

She moves to a door behind us and unlocks it, then opens it and turns on the light. The room is full of stuff: old broken desks, beat-up chairs, and dusty shelves.

For a second I think she gonna lock me in here, that all this was a trick.

"You never know what'll happen when you walk through a new door. It may be a mess at first, but given a good cleaning, it can become something fresh."

I get it. "Is that like, what you call it—a metaphor?"

She shrugs. "Could be. But for now, it's also your punishment. You and those other boys are gonna spend the afternoon cleaning this room out so we can put it to good use. We have a new teacher coming in who wants to start a computer lab."

I sigh, then turn around to see the other boys I fought, standing there too.

She turns to all of us and says, "This is a truce. You'll work together without any more fighting, or you'll have me to deal with. And you *do not* want that."

The nice lady I was talking to is gone, and in her place is the lady I don't wanna mess with. Then the janitor shows up with a cart loaded with mops and brooms and rags and trash cans. We all stand there, looking at each other.

"Well? What are you waiting for? Get to work!"

Principal Butler says. "And just in case you're thinking of messing around, know that I have the basement under the gym that needs sorting—and believe me, you do not want to go down there."

If this door is a opportunity, it sucks.

FIFTEEN

Coach Whitman also seems to have taken a interest in me. Maybe she feels sorry for me 'cause she sees how tired I am by the time I get to the Academy in the afternoons. She keeps showing up with "leftovers" that look like full meals to me. I'm usually starving by then, so I scarf them down, but I don't want her to think I'm some kinda charity case.

"I appreciate your help, Cole," Coach says. "As soon as I get more hands in here, we can ease up a bit on your schedule, since the season won't kick in for a couple months. I know it's hard doing school and working every day. Just let me know if you need help with anything. That includes school."

We start talking about doing a four-day schedule in a week or so. She does not want me to fail out of North, and even suggests I can take advantage of the tutors at the Academy library.

"Really?" I ask.

"Really." She walks me over to the library one day, which opens up into a giant room with columns and statues and loads of books. Students are studying, and some of them look at me funny when we walk up to the tutor's station.

Coach introduces me to a tutor who looks like a perfect student: hair just right, glasses, and pressed pants. He seems to respect Coach, and she leaves me in his hands. But when he takes a look at the bio and world history homework I brought, he makes a sour face.

"This is what you're working on over there?" he asks.

"Yeah . . . ?" I say, not sure if that's a good or bad thing.

He acts like a doctor about to give bad news. "You're going to have to up your game if you want to go to college. Are you taking any AP courses? Don't they have an IB program?"

All them initials don't mean nothing to me. "IB . . . ?"

I look down at the paper. This seem hard enough to me. "I'm pretty sure kids at North go to college . . ." I answer, again not sure.

He takes off his glasses like a professor might and gives me a concerned look. "Look, North is *not* a college prep school." He slides over to his laptop and types away. Now his face looks really concerned. "They rank one out of ten in college readiness."

"Number one sounds pretty good," I say.

"Ten is the high mark. North is in last place in test scores . . . with a forty-six percent suspension rate and a dropout ratio of . . ." He whistles and shakes his head. "Look, Cole. I'm going to be honest with you. I can help you with your homework as a courtesy to Coach Whitman, but . . . I'm not sure that's going to help you much."

He sits back and studies me. "You really should think about coming here instead."

"What, like go to military school?" I glance up at a painting on the wall of Revolutionary soldiers looking all high-and-mighty.

He sees what I'm looking at, then leans in like he don't want the other students to hear. "Don't get caught up in the uniforms and all that, Cole. We're a college prep academy focused on higher learning.

Ninety-eight percent of our graduates go on to college. You'd stand a much better chance at a place like this."

"You have . . . any kids like me here?" I ask.

He knows what I'm on about. "Not many. But if Coach Whitman believes in you, then why not? And we're actually starting a new day school program next year that will be just like high school. No military stuff."

I try to imagine me in this library for real, sitting next to the kids around a desk doing homework. "Yeah? And how much is that?" I ask.

He turns back to his laptop, and types some more. A page comes up with a number: $31,975.

My jaw almost falls off. "For four years of high school?"

He looks taken aback. "No . . . that's *per year*," he says.

I try to do the math, but it's so high, I can't add all them numbers together in my head. "Uh, I live in Strawberry Mansion. You know we ain't rich. I'm pretty sure my dad don't make that kinda scratch, like *ever*."

He sits back, trying to process that. "Okay, well . . . wow. So . . . maybe a scholarship? You play polo, don't you?"

SIXTEEN

Y ou got a visitor."

Tex is standing there as I clean out Boo's hoofs, but I know they always pranking me—and besides, who's gonna visit me here at the Ritz? "If it's the TV news, tell them to get in touch with my people."

He looks back out toward the street. "I don't think she's with the news."

I look at Boo, who suddenly raises his head and starts to move out of his stall. "Boo, hold up—"

He practically knocks me over, but only 'cause he lumbering off.

"Hey, Boo! Remember me?" Ruthie is holding out a big ol' carrot, which Boo devours. "That's right, your old pal Ruthie. *That's right . . . that's right.*"

I hate that my first thought is feeling embarrassed that she's here, wondering what the fellas might think of how she looks and all. But even after I squash that, it's weird seeing her in my world. On top of that, it's even weirder seeing her talk to Boo like he's a baby. "He don't like being talked to like that," I say, dusting myself off.

"No?" She gives him another carrot and does more baby talk. *"That's right, my wittle Boo-Boo. Your auntie Ruth is here now . . ."*

Tex is grinning at the show. "He could use a woman's touch. You the one who took care of him at the other stables?"

"Yes, sir. Name's Ruthie." She shakes Tex's hand, and I'm impressed how he don't flinch or look away from her face but treats her like anyone else. Then, just as I finish that thought, he nods toward her face and says, "So, you always been like that?"

Ruthie glances at me, and I remember her comment about how old people are the worst.

But then he says, "So good with animals, I mean. I can tell a real horse person when I see one."

115

She smiles. "Yes, sir. My mom says animals take to me. In fact, I probably have more friends that are animals than human."

Tex gestures to me. "Well, I guess that's why you like our Cole too. He's kind of our mascot around here."

I push him out gently. "Thanks, Tex. You can go now."

He nudges me back. "I'm just pulling your leg, son." Then he does the baby voice. "We love our *wittle* Cole here. Don't we? *That's right. Who's a good mascot . . . ?*"

I look at Ruthie. "Now look what you started. I'll never hear the end of it."

We stand there, staring at each other, and I feel all awkward. I'm glad she's here, but I want to ask her what she's *doing* here.

"You gonna show me around, or what?" she finally asks, looking up at the massive clouds of cobwebs overhead.

"Sure." I look up. "Oh, *that*? The maid hasn't been in this week yet."

"More like a couple decades," she says.

I show her the other horses and tell her stories about each one—where they came from, what their personalities are like. "They a buncha misfits, but they match Chester Avenue for sure."

When I stop and glance down the row, I can see all the fellas standing there, gaping at us. I give them a look before she sees them, and they nudge each other and mosey off. When we get back to Boo, she asks, "Mind if I take him for a spin? For old times' sake?" I don't know how I feel about that. "He don't like nobody ridin' him but me."

"Oh, he won't mind," she says, and starts putting on his bridle. What's worse is Boo don't even flinch like normal.

"Traitor," I say in his ear.

She starts to lead him out the barn. "What about a saddle?" I ask.

She shrugs it off. "Sometimes it's good to freestyle it."

I watch her lead Boo over to the vacant lot across the street and scramble up on him without a saddle, like it was nothing. The fellas have come back to watch, and Bob whispers in my ear. "Hmm. Looks like a natural."

Before I can comment, he's laughing with the rest of the guys. "Maybe Boo's got himself a girlfriend."

"Everybody got a opinion . . ." I say to no one. I watch Ruthie ride Boo around the lot, stopping and starting, turning in circles like they doing a dance routine. Then she breaks into a full gallop.

I don't know what bothers me more: that she might be as good a rider as me or that Boo looks like he's having more fun with her.

"I guess he knows who butters the bread," Tex says.

"What's that supposed to mean?"

He shrugs. "What do I know? I'm just an old head."

After watching them do a few more laps, I cross the street and motion for Boo to stop. "My turn."

Ruthie smiles, says into Boo's ear: "Just remember who took care of you . . ."

"Funny," I say as she dismounts. "I think he remembers who saved his butt from the meat factory."

I hop on up and decide to show her a thing or two. Even bareback. I notice Bob left out the barrels he was practicing barrel racing with. I whisper into Boo's ear. "Let's show her who the master is!"

"Heyup!" I kick my heels, and we hit a gallop, straight for the barrels. Then we weave in and out like a slalom racer, chasing the cans, as we say. Smooth. Fast. I even do my rodeo spin-the-horn move when I hit the turn, which gotta impress. We run around them a few more times, then I motion to Ruthie like, that's how we do—until Boo suddenly stops, sending me crashing into his neck and almost off his back. When I look down, I see a plastic bag blowing by.

Ruthie looks amused.

"Boo, you makin' me look bad," I hiss in his ear, then smile and nod to Ruthie like it was nothing. We trot up to where she's sitting on the fence, checking out the spread.

"You know what this field would be good for?"

I'm thinking that it's already good for *us*. But then she says, "Polo."

I kinda chuckle, then look back at the guys kicking back under the tent, drinking beers and talking smack.

"Uh, yeah, I don't think polo's gonna fly on Chester

Ave." But she's off again, walking the field, moving some barrels around.

"Uh, don't do that!" I yell to her. "Bob wants them there like—"

She ignores me. "Grab those boxes and move them over there."

"Yeah, but . . ." She's moving things around, all the while marching like a toy soldier around the perimeter.

"What are you doin'?" I ask.

"Measuring."

I look over at the guys, who are all watching her and making comments to each other. "Measurin' what?" I ask.

"The field. Not quite as big as our arena, but we can do, like, a hundred fifty by seventy-five feet or something, just to keep it easy."

She marks the corners and goals. Next thing I know, she's running over to the bike she rode over, which has a big bag draped across the bars. She pulls out some mallets and starts walking straight over to the guys!

"No . . . hold up. Ruthie!" I shout.

Too late. By the time I get there, she's all into it. "It's like playing soccer. But on a horse, you know? Any of you know how to rodeo?"

They all looking at her like she cray-cray. Tex raises his hand. "Did twenty years on the circuit."

She grins. "Good, good. Rodeoing helps. You need good hand-eye coordination. We can start off easy, just playing on foot. But we need at least four others . . ." She looks at them like they all gonna stand up and volunteer.

They all look at me, and I just shrug. "I told you they'd—"

"Can we play?"

We glance over and see two of the neighborhood kids, Lil' C-Jay and P'nut, kicking back on a old La-Z-Boy chair. They both ten and think they can ride with the best of us, even if they just shorties with no fear.

"Sure! Come on." She hands them two shorter mallets. "We'll start off two on two. I'm sure a couple of these guys will join in later. If they can get off their rocking chairs . . ."

They make faces at each other. Nothing like a good smackdown.

Jamaica Bob chuckles. "Cowboy polo. This should be good."

SEVENTEEN

Cowboy polo was more fun than I wanted to admit. Ruthie started coming by a coupla nights a week and teaching us the fundamentals. We were mostly on foot, playing with shorter sticks she called foot mallets. Sometimes we played on bikes too, but even without horses, Ruthie's a stickler for the rules. She taught us some basic strategy, about fouls and penalties, handicaps. She even made me carry around a tennis ball so I could squeeze it during the day to make my wrist and grip stronger.

Sometimes I stayed late at the Academy after the Generals went off to dinner, and me and Ruthie would play one-on-one in the arena. She showed me how to maneuver, polo-style, using voice commands and shifting my weight with my feet, knees, even my fingers.

"When you get good, ponies will follow your lead when you just look or think something. Like mind-melding—use your brain, and they pick up on your thoughts."

"Okay, Professor X."

"Don't laugh, Cole. I've seen Coach do it. She just looks in a direction, and her pony goes there. She thinks, *Stop*, and her pony stops. Sometimes she listens to music with her earbuds, and I swear, her pony starts grooving to the beat. She calls it horse listening."

Me and Boo been together a while, so I know there's something to that. I'd watch his ears perk up, and he'd respond to my little moves and sounds. During drills, I'd try to mind-meld with him as we'd canter, stop, quick turn, move sideways, explode forward, roll back, stop. I was starting to think maybe he *could* feel my thoughts.

For fun, we'd play Capture the Flag or tag on

horseback. But then Ruthie would sneak in drills with funny names: Drop a Stirrup, Stop in a Box, Sit-a-Buck, Grab Your Toe. Mostly Follow-the-Leader, where I just do everything she do. Ruthie told me most of their ponies were mares, because females were better for polo. "They don't quit on you. No matter what, they'll keep going," she said, like she was talking about herself. We'd spend time talking about the different ponies in the barn, and she'd make me lay down on their backs so they could get used to me.

"A polo player has to switch ponies every chukker, so you don't wanna get up on one you haven't met. They have to trust you won't hurt them. And if you can lie on them on your *back*, then you start trusting them."

We were spending a lot of time on polo, so I thought I'd even things out and take her on one of our horses and show her my secret trails in the park, or I'd teach her how to stand on horseback like we do. She fell off a few times, but so did I when she taught me how to lean off my pony to reach for a polo ball and smack it.

We was getting to be friends, but I wasn't sure how Harp would react to Ruthie being at the Ritz. He'd been working a lot, taking whatever jobs he can to make ends meet, from construction to cleaning out sewage tanks to being an assistant to old people. So he's usually not in a good mood when he shows up, but that first time, when he saw Ruthie, he seemed kinda surprised. I wasn't sure if it was 'cause a how she looked or just that there was a girl in the barn to see *me*. But Ruthie charmed him, and he eased up, and even invited her to go on a ride with us.

There's something about riding in a posse. To have your crew with you feels good, and to have Ruthie there somehow made it feel better. It was only then that she got the cowboy thing: She saw how people smile when they see a group of us pass. How little kids look up and point with wonder in their eyes. How girls stop what they doing and whisper to each other. Even how the gangs respect you, 'cause they have to look up to you when you on a horse. I doubt she gets that feeling when she with the Generals.

When we got into Fairmount Park, we let it fly, galloping freely like it was the Old West. We wandered the trails, disappeared into the forest, watered our horses at the creek like the old days. After Harp saw Ruthie could handle herself on a horse, he opened up to her in a way I ain't seen before, even with me.

He even *smiled*.

Whatever else was going on, it didn't matter. When you a cowboy, all is good with the world.

I didn't know where this was going, but after a few weeks, I realized, she was, like, my only friend. The fellas at the Ritz made fun of me for playing polo, asking if I was a real cowboy or not. The cavalry boys made fun of us, asking if she was getting too cowboy to play at the Academy. All I knew was, we was getting good at both.

EIGHTEEN

So, there's a clinic coming up this weekend," Ruthie says to me late one afternoon. It's nearing sunset on Chester Avenue, and the shadows stretch long over the vacant lot. The fellas are away at a horse auction, so it's just me an' her and Lil' C-Jay messing around in a one-on-one-on-one version of cowboy polo.

"What do I need a clinic for? I ain't sick," I say.

"It's not that kind of clinic, dummy," she says. "It's an annual event the Academy throws for sponsors and local booster clubs. A learning clinic. You know, a day when we give back to the community. We'll do training exercises and polo drills for folks who support us."

"Why you tellin' me, then?"

She smiles slyly. "Well, you'll probably be there helping out anyways, but I was thinking maybe doing the drills in the arena with all the proper gear and everything might be good for you."

Sound like more than a suggestion. "Oh, you do? You sayin' I ain't got skills?" I ask.

"Train got mad skills," says C-Jay.

"Thanks, little dude. See?" I say. "I got mad skills."

Ruthie shakes her head. "You know what I mean. Here, we're just playing around. At a clinic, you might get your chance to show some people what you got." Then she says, "And maybe there'll be some press there."

She tosses that off like it's nothing, but I know she's saying it 'cause she thinks I liked being in the news before.

But I'm thinking a good news story might help my chances of getting a scholarship.

"And my mom will be there too. You can meet her," Ruthie adds.

"Your mom?" I know she already met Harp and all, but something about the way she says it makes me feel like I'm being set up or something. But it seems more important to her than she's letting on, so I say, "Okay."

"Can I be part of the press? I know how to work a camera. I'll make you look *good!*" says C-Jay.

"Sorry, you're still too young. Maybe in a couple years," she says.

"Won't Maverick and them be looking for a chance to show us up in front of everybody?" I ask.

She shrugs. "Yeah, but they'll keep it under control. Coach'll be there schmoozing with the booster club supporters and sponsors. You can show *them* what you got. They're the ones who make things happen."

It seem stupid, but now she got me thinking more about that scholarship thing for the Academy. Even I know stuff happens when people with money take a interest. Maybe it might be a good thing to show off my skills. Even if I'm still learning polo, I'm better on horse than some of the Generals. And if somebody took notice, who knows where that might lead? Anything's better than going to North.

Ruthie's leading me and C-Jay through a two-rider drill, me on Boo and C-Jay on his bike, where we're passing a ball forward and back while riding up and down the field, when I look over and see Smush standing there watching us.

"Whatchou doin', cuz?" he asks.

I ain't seen him since our falling-out, but he looks small standing there at the edge of the field all alone.

I don't know how long he's been watching us, but he steps forward and, like a little kid, asks, "Can I play?"

I can see he's trying to smooth things out, but I ain't biting. "You don't even know what we're doin', Smush."

Then he sees Ruthie carrying a few balls back to us and smiles like he knows what time it is. "Oh, I know exactly what you *doing*, cuz . . ."

Ruthie looks over and smiles too. "You ride?"

I laugh, but Smush keeps coming. "Train thinks it's funny 'cause he ain't been around here long enough to remember the legend of Smush when it comes to horse racing."

"I remember one race pretty good," I say, glaring at him. "But we wasn't on no horses."

He sighs, brushes me off. "Get me a horse, and I'll show you what's up."

Ruthie jumps in. "Why not? We can always use another player."

I tense up, try to derail her. "Yeah, I don't think that's a good idea . . ."

Smush is all smiles and walks right up to Ruthie. I worry he's gonna say something dumb about her face, but what he ends up saying is worse: "So, you the one he been goin' on about, gettin' all mushy-eyed over—"

I know it's a play and the only way he'll shut up is for me to give in. "Fine—go get a horse and show us what you got, *cuz*."

He beams and runs off. We watch him disappear into the Ritz.

"He really your cousin?" Ruthie asks.

"Yup."

"You really get mushy—?"

I cut her off. "He means good, but you can't trust anything he says."

"Really? *Nothing?*" she asks.

I feel my face getting all hot. I look at C-Jay, and he makes a little kissing face.

Smush comes back out with, of all horses, *Harp's* horse, Lightning. I freak. "Smush, you know Harp don't like anyone messing with his horse—"

He cuts me off. "*I'm* the one who found this horse, so technically, he's *mine*."

"Wait—what do you mean, *you* found this horse? Harp acts like he gave birth to Lightning or somethin'."

He strokes Lightning's neck, and Lightning seems to approve. "I don't know about that, but I went to one of them horse auctions with Tex a few years back, and guys was gettin' their horses ready to show them off. Tex was goin' on about how most of 'em was gonna end up dog food and whatnot, 'cause they was worthless to the race trainers after a certain age. But there was fire in this one horse, I tell you that."

"What do you know about fire?" I ask.

He gives me a look. "I know attitude. I know fight, 'cause I got plenty of that. I could see he had plenty of life in him. He was just rough around the edges. He even had this dope lightning bolt patch on his head. I thought, *That's the one*."

"See? He's a real horse lover," says Ruthie.

"I only seen him on a horse once, and that was on a rescue mission," I say.

Smush nods. "True that. But when you stay with Harp, he's gonna work you, and that means horses."

"Wait, you stayed here too?" I asked. "What else you hidin'?"

"I ain't hiding nothin', cuz. Just tellin' it how it was. I didn't have no money, but Tex musta seen me havin' a moment with Lightning, 'cause next thing I know, he bought him. Then he just handed me the reins and said, 'A man is only as good as his horse!' And you don't know this, 'cause you wasn't around then, but I trained this horse. I mean, with Harp's help. But he was mine. And I rode him good. Even beat Harp once at the Speedway."

"I knew you was lyin'. Then how come he's Harp's horse now?" I ask.

His face grows dark. He shrugs. "I got involved in other stuff is all. Hell, I was fifteen, what do you expect? I guess I wandered too far for Harp's liking, and next thing I knew, he kicked me out and took over Lightning, and that was that."

There's a long pause. I feel bad for him, even though I know it was his own dang fault.

"Well, you're here now," says Ruthie. "So if you want to learn a little polo, I can show you a thing or two."

Smush looks up and smiles at me. "I knew she was good people."

Ruthie looks at me to see if it's cool. I nod. As long as Harp don't show up, I guess.

I watch as Ruthie shows Smush a few basics. She don't know him like I do, but I guess I don't know him like I thought I did neither. And it turns out, he can ride. We mess around for a few hours, practicing swings and maneuvers, but I keep a eye out for Harp's truck so there won't be any fireworks. We have us some fun, and Smush looks like he's into it. I'm still not so sure why he's here, but he seem to be trying to make things right.

As we're putting things away, Ruthie pats Smush on the shoulder. I hear her saying how he had good energy out there, and he acts all shy, grinning like he won the spelling bee. Then he tells her he used to feel like Lightning could read his thoughts and that tonight he felt like his horse remembered him. I can tell Ruthie's a sucker for that kinda thing, 'cause she says, "You know, there's a polo clinic we're putting on to this weekend. Maybe you—"

I rush in. "No, no, Ruthie. That's cool. It's not really his thing. Besides, ain't it for the school supporters?" The last thing I need is Smush there, embarrassing me.

Smush sees what I'm doing. "You know, maybe I *will* go . . . I'd really like to learn more."

I look at him, and I know he's just winding me up. So I wind him up too. "Okay. Yeah, whatever, cuz. You *should* come. There'll be lots of people there, and I think polo could really be your thing. Maybe you'll even find some new *customers* . . ."

Smush doesn't say anything, but he knows what I'm talking about. He looks down, nods, and quietly takes Lightning back to his stall. I can see Ruthie giving me a look, like *I'm* the bad guy. The silence is getting to me, so I go after him and find him in the barn.

"Don't worry about it, Smush. Come watch if you want, but you don't gotta," I say.

He nods. We bump fists, and he heads out. "It was good to meet ya, Ruthie. Keep an eye on my boy here. Sometimes he don't like to share. But with you, I understand."

We watch him go. I can feel Ruthie wanting to say something, but I say it first. "It was nice of you to invite him. But that really ain't his world."

NINETEEN

B oo!" Coach cries out as soon as she sees me ride into
the arena on Community Polo Day. She strokes his
head, and he seem happy to be back. "We miss having
him here. Glad you brought him, Cole."

"It was Ruthie's idea," I say. "She thought it'd be
good to have him mix with the other ponies."

"Well, I'm glad. I hear she's been training you too."
She nudges me.

"Yeah, I'm not sure you can take the cowboy outta
the rider," I say. "We been playin' the cowboy version,
I guess."

"Well, I'm happy you're here. We'll need your help tacking up the ponies and helping with the equipment, but otherwise, feel free to participate."

I nod, but I also check out the scene to see who I might need to impress. "I heard there might be press here?" I say, looking around.

She laughs. "Well, I suppose Ronnie is our pressman today. He's live-streaming and posting pics to our social-media platforms."

Ronnie? I spot the plebe filming on his iPhone. When his camera catches us, he smiles and waves. Not exactly ESPN, but I guess getting my mug all over the Academy's Instagram feed is the next best thing for getting noticed. As long as I'm not embarrassed in public.

I wave at Ronnie and ride over to say hi. He takes my pic on Boo. "Do me a favor, will ya?" I say. "If you get any good shots of me showin' off, be sure to post them, okay? My mama lives outta town, and she never seen me do this kinda thing before."

"Sure thing, Cole. My mom loves seeing me on the Facebook feed. 'Course it helps when you're the one taking the pictures and you throw in a selfie now and then." He winks.

I see my in. "Hey, maybe we do a selfie for both our moms?" I dismount, put my arm around him.

Click. He uploads it. First post of Polo Day at the Academy: me and my man Ronnie.

"Well, I see you met the media." I look up and see Ruthie, dressed in her best polo gear, on Patches, who's all groomed and pretty. Ruthie's looking pretty good herself in them threads.

"Yeah, Ronnie here works for *Sports Illustrated.* He promised me the cover," I say.

"What?" says Ronnie, oblivious. "We were just taking pics for our mommies."

"Oh, isn't *that* cute," Ruthie says. "Speaking of moms, maybe . . . you wanna meet mine?" She nods toward the stands, where a group of supporters are all gathered around a older guy who I recognize as the commander. He's dressed in camo, not in his fancy uniform. It looks like what he'd wear in wartime. He's holding on to the biggest horse I've seen here, a seventeen-hander.

"The commander plays polo?" I ask.

"No, but he started the C Troop here back in the day. Sometimes he likes to ride with us."

"Hey, which one's your moms?" I ask.

"Who do you think?" she asks.

Of the twenty or so supporters, only one is black. I guess I was expecting her to look like Ruthie, but her skin seem normal. In fact, as far as moms go, she's kinda, well . . . "The one that looks like Beyoncé?"

Ruthie elbows me in the side.

"What? She does!"

We ride over toward her, Ronnie following. Ruthie's mom glances over and sees her coming. All smiles—till she sees *me*, then a look of suspicion clouds her eyes.

"I can tell she likes me already," I say through my teeth.

"*Shut up,*" Ruthie hisses. She waves. "Hi, Mom!"

"You're looking sharp, honey." She hugs her daughter while keeping a eye on me. "And who is this?"

I introduce myself before Ruthie says anything. "Hi. I'm Cole. I take care of the ponies around here."

I can see she don't quite approve of me—until Ruthie calls her on it. "Mom!"

Ruthie's mom breaks into a smile. "Hi, Cole. I'm just messing with you to embarrass my daughter in front of her friends." She reaches out and hugs me while Ronnie gets it all on video. "I hear you're a cowboy?"

"Yes, ma'am, I guess I am. But I'm just here to help."

"Ruthie tells me you're angling to get into the school," she says, sounding excited. I look at Ruthie. News to me.

"Um . . ."

Her mom nods. "Don't be shy. We're always on the lookout for fresh recruits, and between us, it'd be nice to get some more POCs in here."

POCs? Ruthie whispers in my ear: "People Of Color." Oh.

Before I can say anything, her mother asks, "Have you met the commander?"

Next thing I know, I'm shaking hands with the head of the school, and all I'm thinking is, I never met a commander before. "Cole here helped save his community from developers," says Ruthie's mom, like she knows all about me. "He was on the news."

"Is that so?" says the commander. "Are you a member of polo squad?"

I grin and look around to see if anyone on the polo team mighta heard his mistake. "No, sir. I help take care of the ponies."

Ruthie's mom continues to talk about me, and the commander nods, but all I'm noticing is Ruthie and how she's looking at me being all nice with her mom and the head of the school. Kinda like she's impressed.

"Commander, sir, how about a picture?" says Ronnie. Perfect timing. Second post: me with the commander, Ruthie, and her mom.

TWENTY

Coach waves us over, and Ruthie and me head into the center of the arena, along with about fifteen other people in horse wear. Some have polo outfits. Others, like me, is dressed in jeans and Ts. Some are college age, some look like parents, and there's a couple old heads. All are white.

I see the Generals spread out in different parts of the arena, prepping their stations. Maverick is putting a saddle on a wood horse. Bandit is laying down a few chalk lines leading to the goal. Brick is talking to the gray-haired couple and looking like he wishes he was somewhere else.

"So, what are *you* gonna teach us?" I ask Ruthie.

"I'm gonna school you, is what. You'll see. Maybe Boo'll want to stay at the end of the day."

"Doubt it. He has too much self-respect."

Coach blows her whistle as she rides into the center of the ring. "Gather 'round, everybody!" We all wander over around Coach. I bring Boo along.

"Welcome to our twelfth annual Community Polo Clinic, where we get to give something back to our friends and followers who have supported our program these past many years," says Coach. "Some of you have been playing polo for a while, and some of you are beginners, but I know all of you love the sport, and we wouldn't have these great ponies here without your support, so thank you!"

Everyone claps, all smiles. Then—

"Hey!" someone shouts from outside. Everyone turns toward the barn door, and next thing I know, Smush rushes in, followed by one of the junior cadet guards, who's yelling, "Hey, stop!"

"Relax, man, I was invited." Smush sees us all looking his way. He grins. "'Sup, cuz! Ruthie. Sorry I'm late!"

Coach looks at me and Ruthie, who shrugs. "I did invite him. He's one of my . . . trainees?"

143

Smush goes right up and shakes Coach's hand. "Cool. Name's Smush. Big fan of polo. Got all the shirts." He's actually wearing a brand-new Ralph Lauren polo shirt and jeans.

Brick rolls his eyes and whispers some comment to the others, who laugh.

"Welcome, Smoosh," says Coach. "We just got started."

He comes and stands next to me and daps as he says "'Sup, cuz." He looks over at Brick's red hair. "Whoa, wassup, Ron Weasley? You got big!" Bandit laughs, but Brick stares him down.

"Really?" I say to Smush.

He grins. "Hey, man, if you gonna do somethin', go all in."

Coach introduces Maverick and the team, who are gonna act like teachers today so they can pass on all they've learned. "Here at the Academy, we use polo to improve riding skills and teach leadership, teamwork, and strategy. So the team will be leading the different stations today, with a little assistance from me and a few professionals from the Polo Club."

Coach divides everyone into three groups. I have Smush in mine, along with the older couple, Tim and Regan, who live in the Heights. When they mention they're neighbors of Ruthie's, I look over at her mom, who, I realize, is dressed like money. Then I notice a banner on the wall behind her, with her picture on it, as a sponsor of the upcoming season.

Is Ruthie, like, rich?

But before I wonder too much about that, Regan asks me where I'm from, and I say Strawberry Mansion. That ends the small talk.

Coach pulls me aside for a second and asks me to help out as I move from station to station—tacking ponies, collecting balls, and fetching mallets and stuff, which I'm cool with. Seems like there's time to better my skills and help out too.

The first station we go to is Ruthie's, and she's manning the wood horse, which is actually a proper wood horse and not that sawhorse thing Ruthie was using back at the police barn, and is sitting in what looks like a batting cage. "You didn't tell me you live in the Heights," I say to her on the sly.

She acts like I spit on her or something. "Oh, you gonna judge me?" she whispers, eyeing Brick and Bandit. "We worked hard to get here. Nobody gave us anything."

Whoa. I can see I pushed a button for her. "Jeez, sorry. I didn't mean nothin' by it." She watches me as I back off with the others. She takes a breath to gather herself and starts her spiel, all smiles.

"Welcome to my station," she says. "This morning, we're going to focus on refining our hit points, both offside and nearside, and fore and back swings." She demonstrates while standing, swinging her arms on the left and right, forward and back. "And we're going to practice hitting away from your pony for open shots, and how to execute a good tail shot, or under-the-neck shot. Basic, I know, but as Coach says: you can't over-practice the fundamentals."

She gets up on the wood horse and gives a little demo of swings, pointing out how important it is to hit the ball *slowly*. "Almost everyone hits too hard in the beginning. That's how you hurt your wrist and miss the ball. Remember, the faster you are riding, the slower you swing, the farther the ball will go."

She yells *giddyup*, and everyone laughs, 'cause, of course, the wood horse don't move.

The old couple seem glued to her every word, but then I notice the old guy is staring at her face most the time, to the point where his wife nudges him. I know Ruthie sees, but she just keeps going like a pro. It's actually kinda cool seeing her as the teacher.

"Any questions so far?" she asks.

"I got a question," I say, being the smart-ass. "What's a chukkerhead?"

She laughs, so I guess we're cool. "A chukkerhead is someone who lives and breathes polo. Like me. Now, a *knucklehead* is something else," she says, looking at me. I hold up my hands.

Smush is quiet and glued to her every word. I don't know what's up with him or why he's taken a interest in polo, of all things. Maybe our close call with death shook him up some and he's actually changed and is trying to reconnect or something. I keep looking at him sideways, but he's hard to read. When Ruthie asks for her first victim, I'm surprised Smush volunteers.

"Sure that pony ain't gonna buck me?" he jokes.

When he gets up on the wood horse, all grins, he pretends to be a rodeo rider for a second.

"Let's try a nice easy forehand strike," says Ruthie.

Ruthie puts the ball down offside. Smush lines up the shot with his mallet, winds up, and lets it fly, but he muffs it and it sails off to the side.

"Slooow," Ruthie says. She watches him do a couple more, then goes up and gives him a little adjustment and shows him how to lead with his mallet and not his hand. "Try not to flatten the mallet on your downswing." She makes a few corrections with Smush's arm but does it in a way that never makes him look bad. "Try it again," she says.

He does and hits it straight into the target. The older couple clap. Smush too. "Nice one, Smush!" Ruthie says.

I've been helping out at each station like Coach asked, but when Smush and me move to Brick's station, he takes it to the next level, making me demonstrate on a pony how to stand in the stirrups, trying to put me in my place.

"*Lift* that butt out of the saddle for your half-seat position!" Brick yells at me. "Turn your *shoulders* so that they are *parallel* to the horse! *Extend* your arm all the way back so your elbow is *straight*! Keep your head over the ball!" He rides me like a drill sergeant, pointing at me like I'm a specimen in some museum. But I refuse to show him my pain. I hold the poses till my arms or legs is about to fall off, but Smush don't appreciate that and starts making little comments back at Brick. I give him a look that says, *Stand down*.

We spend the next few hours going station to station. I help with all the ponies, getting people up and down from their mounts, switching out rides for rest, handing out mallets, and placing balls. We practice how to warm up a horse for playing: slow cantering to the right, stopping and starting, quick turns, trotting and sprinting to blow the horse's nose out for good breathing. Then we hit the drills: We do circle taps, circling around a ball and tapping it over and over. We do two-rider drills, passing the ball forward, then leaving it for the second rider to hit it up to you. We practice two-handed stops, putting our weight in the stirrup on the side of the horse we hit from, even riding without stirrups to strengthen our legs.

Smush is starting to get impatient. "When we gonna play some ball, cuz? This is for suckers, man. All they do is point us out, like that's how *not* to do it. Treatin' me like I'm some beginner who don't know squat."

I don't say the obvious. "You wanted to be here, Smush. Me, I'm workin'." And I am.

"They treatin' you with no respect, cuz."

But I'm trying to make good in front of Ruthie and her mom. They got me thinking about making a good impression. So I work hard, show off some skills on horseback, and refuse to let the guys get the better of me.

At Maverick's station, he rides his pony back and forth like he's really a general or something. He points his mallet at each one of us as he makes his points. "Welcome to the Ten Commandments of Polo!"

Great, now he thinks he Moses.

TWENTY-ONE

LINE—MAN—BALL: the first commandment of polo!" Maverick shouts. "A player must learn *not* to chase the ball but to play your man! What's the line of the ball?" he asks, looking at us.

Even I know this by now: "It's like the line the ball makes when you hit it," I say. "It makes a line in the road—everyone's gotta stay on one side or the other, or they start crashin' into each other."

"That's downright poetic, Cole. What he means is, when you hit a moving ball to where it stops, it creates an invisible line that can't be crossed from any direction. Cross it, and it's a foul. So, what does Line-Man-Ball mean?"

Tim raises his hand. "Know where the opposition is, determine the line of their ball to avoid crossing it for a foul, *then* attack the ball!" says Tim.

"Very good, sir. So, if you find yourself all alone on the polo field, you're in the wrong place!" He's looking at me, but I just stare back.

He moves his pony in a circle, glancing all around him. "Polo is a game of anticipation and communication. Anticipate the action and call it out. When you are behind your teammate and he is about to hit a backhand, you can call to him, "Open shot!" or "Tail it!" to tell him where the shot is. Your head should be on a swivel at all the times, looking behind you to anticipate the coming shot or forward to call out where the shot is going."

He has us running on our feet with shorter foot mallets, moving and calling out shots as we pass the ball forward and back.

"Tail!" shouts Tim. Regan passes it back to him, and I call out "Open!" and he takes the open shot to goal.

"Good! Playing the angles is about covering the spread of the field. But the most powerful way to the goal is to ride the train," Maverick says, shooting me a look. "What's the train, Train?"

He puts me on the spot, but I got this, 'cause Ruthie taught me a thing or two. "The train is about lining up, one, two, three, equal distance from your teammate," I say. "The number three can pass forward to the two. The two can pass up to the one. If the one misses, then the two is already in line to ride up and get the ball. If the two misses, then the three's right there to follow up."

He knows I'm right, so he barely acknowledges my answer. Instead he plows through the rest of his strategies as he makes me run around as a example: "Keep *possession* of the ball! *Think* before hitting. Don't just hit it away, or you're giving the *other team* a chance to get the ball." He takes a few short swings, then eases it into the goal. Then he turns and rides the ball back toward me.

"The *attitude* of the players attacking versus those defending is different!" he shouts. "Except for this: Play defense as hard as you play offense, because a goal *saved* is the same as a goal *scored*."

He rides the ball right by me, expecting me to make a play, but I ain't stupid. I'm on foot and have no chance. So I just stand there and let him pass.

Smush walks up to me as Maverick shoots and scores. "Dang, do he really think like that's some big reveal, cuz? Any fool knows that you gotta attack and defend. He's just showing you up, man. Why you put up with that?"

When Maverick comes back around, Smush makes himself heard. "Yo, man, what's up, fella? Why you runnin' my boy so hard? Put him on his horse and he'll show you that attitude."

"Pony," says Maverick.

"What's that?" says Smush, pretending he didn't hear.

"We call them ponies. This isn't the rodeo, *fella*."

The older couple is looking uncomfortable, but Smush isn't one to back down. "'Fella'? Say, Cole told me that y'all have to salute any visitors in your presence and call them *sir*. That true?"

Smush waits. Maverick looks to the others but still doesn't salute Smush. "I like to show respect to those that deserve it, sir. But we still call them ponies."

Smush nods. "Ponies, huh? Kinda like at the state fair, am I right?"

"Technically, sir. Polo ponies—"

"That's all right, Major Man. At ease and carry on," says Smush. "But let me be your next example. I'll show you what's up."

I whisper to Smush to go easy. He looks at me. "Workin' for them is cool, but don't ever let them treat you like you they boy. You *my* boy, remember that."

Coach is the first one to get us all up on the ponies, and she's set up a situation where we're supposed to find the line of the ball and take it downfield to the goal. She's on her pony, putting pressure on us the whole way. I'm on Boo, who, thanks to Ruthie's training, manages to outrun Coach's attempts at bumping me from my line of attack. I even out-hustle Brick and tap it into the goal. Ronnie gets it all on video, giving me a big thumbs-up as I ride back around.

"Nice one, Cole," says Coach. "There might be a polo player in you yet."

Ruthie's been watching me. She gives me a nod, which turns into a grin when I hold my mallet up in victory.

After a few hours of running drills, we take a break, and Ruthie asks me if I can help her a minute. Food and drinks have been put out, which gets my attention, but Ruthie pulls me aside, into a tack room.

"What is it? I'm hungry," I say. "They been workin' me hard."

"I know. I been keeping an eye on you."

She has a strange look in her eye, and she's almost making me blush. "Okay, well, what do you need? You want me to carry something like the others been makin' me do?"

She turns and faces me. "No. Just wanted to thank you."

I stop and look at her. "Um . . . okay?"

"No, really," she says. "I know I dragged you here, and I kind of pulled Smush in even after you didn't want me to, and I know Brick and them don't make your life easy."

I'm hearing her, but her words is kinda going out the window, 'cause she's inching toward me till we're suddenly standing face-to-face, and my heart is beating fast and I've stopped thinking about food, even though I got this weird feeling in my stomach, and the next thing I know—we're kissing.

My mind goes blank, and this warm feeling washes over me like the ocean, and I feel light and buzzing all over. We pull back an inch, and I look deep into her eyes. *You're welcome* is what I wanna say, but I don't think anything comes out of my mouth. I notice I got my arms wrapped around her and hers wrapped around me, and I don't care if Smush or even her mom is right outside this door. Nothing is gonna ruin this moment.

Then I hear: "Oh, man, this is even better than I thought." I look over and see Brick holding out his phone as he records us.

Correction. There *is* something that can ruin this moment, and I'm looking at it.

TWENTY-TWO

I notice the Generals is having a good laugh over Brick's video as I head back at the end of the break. I try to play it cool, but I also avoid Ruthie 'cause of it, and I can see it bothers her too. That's the kinda viral post I'm hoping don't make it onto social media.

After the break, the Generals and a few of Coach's polo friends from a nearby club put on some demonstration chukkers for us. Coach does the play-by-play, pointing out what's happening, different strategies, and why and how someone scores or defends. "It's all about finding the ebb and flow of the game in the rhythms of the other ponies. They'll naturally move in packs, like a flock of birds. If your team can play as one, you start to move as one, and then everything else will fall into place."

The dust flies, and the horses thunder. I notice each player has their own style and swagger. But when they play as one, goals happen. The Generals hold their own, but the pros get the better of them, and Smush makes sure the Generals hear it, booing every time they score.

"Pretty soon, we gonna be doin' that to them," he says, all cocky. That might be a long way off.

Then it's time for a match, to "get us used to the action," Coach says. First up is gonna be me, Tim, and Regan against Maverick, Bandit, and Ruthie. I have to change into full polo gear: helmet, leather elbow and knee pads, gloves, equestrian boots, and white pants.

Smush gives me a hard time. "You gonna wear those tight pants, cuz? Can't wait till the guys see the video."

I turn and see Ruthie leading Boo to me, only Boo looks like he's had a makeover. His mane and tail is braided tight and he's got on pink shin wraps.

"Oh, now we talkin'," says Smush. "Boo and you make quite the couple."

"Cadet Spots, let's get this demo going," says Maverick.

He turns to me. "Coach asked us to go easy on the geriatrics. You, however, will get the full treatment."

"You don't scare me, Maverick," I say.

"It's First Lieutenant, plebe. And you *should* be scared. Maybe with that Northside education of yours, you just don't know any better."

He trots off, and Ruthie gives me a *Sorry* look before following. I know this is just practice, but I also know I got to prove myself. Not only to the Generals, but to Coach and the others too. If for nothing else, just to show I can hold my own.

A few minutes later, the six of us players line up for a face-off in the middle of the arena. This feels really different than messing around with cowboy polo back on Chester Ave. Wearing a helmet and all this armor reminds me of some King Arthur story—like we knights getting ready to joust or something.

Maverick shakes hands with Tim, grinning ear to ear. "Good luck out there, sir. Give it your best shot. We appreciate all your support!"

"It's our pleasure, young man. You have a bright future ahead of you," Tim says.

I can see how Maverick looks to the outside world. When he wants to be, he is respectful, and he's strong and looks great in the uniform. He's the young leader type the Academy wants to promote.

Barf.

I fist-bump everyone, and when I get to Ruthie,

she gives me a cold stare. "For now, you're the enemy," she says. Then she winks. "Boo, just remember: When Mama comes running downfield, get out the way."

I look Boo in the eye. "Boo, if it comes down to her and me, just remember who kept you from becomin' dog food."

Boo snorts. He ain't having none of it.

"The TRAIN!" shouts Smush. "Wooo-woooo! He gives me a standing O from the sidelines and boos the Generals when they line up.

I tighten my grip on the mallet. Coach throws in the ball, and Tim gets to it first and establishes his line of play. I see Regan spread to the wing, and Tim taps her a pass, which she *tap-tap-taps* into the goal. They high-five.

"Nice!" Coach claps. Maverick smiles. I know he went easy on them.

We switch goals, and the ball is thrown in, and this time, Maverick gets the jump on Tim and sends it sailing over Regan's head. I'm there, ready for it, but suddenly Bandit's got a line on it and gets control. Boo's out of position, and turning him around almost sends me flying off. Bandit tries to thread the ball through Boo's legs, and Boo accidentally kicks it into the goal! When Bandit canters back past me, he tips his helmet. "Nice D, Train."

They score two more goals on me, rubbing it in for real, even slamming the ball off my leg one time. Coach misses it. "How is that not a foul?" I shout as Maverick scores.

"You'll know when I foul you, Train," he says.

The next series, he plays nice, letting Tim get a shot in. Tim is happy. The Generals score two more times 'cause Tim and Regan are worthless when it comes to defending, leaving me outnumbered. Both times they charge me, two-on-one, and all I got is my mallet to block a shot with. But with a minute to go, Tim is getting tired, and he waves me over. "You play number one. Get a score for yourself, okay?" I like the sound of that.

When Bandit notices me changing to the number one jersey, he's grinning. I can't help myself—I got too much playground moves for my own good. "Game on, boys," I say.

Maverick looks at Bandit. "Sounds like he means business."

"I'm shaking," says Bandit.

Before I can say anything else, Coach throws the ball in, and Maverick steals it from under Boo's nose. "Too slow," I hear him say, and he's off.

I turn Boo around and pursue. Regan surprises

me by coming up on Maverick and knocking him off his line into the wall, hockey-style! There's a scramble, then Tim finds the ball and whacks it over Maverick's head and straight to me!

Bandit's on the other side of the ring, and the ball bounces under Boo. "Neck!" shouts Tim, and Boo turns, and suddenly I got a clean neck shot into an open line of play. There's no one between me and the goal, but right when I line up a shot, I glance up and see Ruthie running at me, crouched with her mallet held high. I swing, but Ruthie blocks my mallet with hers and the ball skitters off Boo's hoof, right between me and a rushing Bandit.

Ruthie has a look of satisfaction in her eyes, but I just want that ball before Bandit gets it, so I tear my mallet away and pull Boo hard off Ruthie, and next thing I see is Bandit's horse coming straight up on Boo.

And then I'm airborne.

TWENTY-THREE

One thing that's always scared me about horses: the thought of a thousand-pound beast stomping on my head.

So imagine what it was like opening my eyes from the ground with four horses stomping all around me in a frenzy. That's where I find myself, and unlike last time when the Generals were messing with me, this feels way more out of control.

WHOMP!

A hoof misses my head by a coupla inches.

WHOMP!

Another one on the other side of my head. I curl up into a ball, trying to protect myself. Dirt is flying in my eyes, and I can't really see anything but white spots, and I'm all dizzy and not thinking straight, but I do know this: I am looking up at the belly of a beast. There are horses all over me and voices yelling, and I think, *This is it: this is how I die.*

Next thing I know, the sky opens up and someone pulls me out—Smush.

He drags me into the clear and pulls off my helmet to get a good look at me. "Cuz! Cuz, you all right?"

His voice seems far off, and I turn away 'cause I think I'm gonna throw up. I retch but nothing comes out. When I open my eyes, I see Smush going toe to toe with Bandit. Maverick and Ruthie are trying to pull them apart, and the others are either pulling their horses away or trying to catch the few who are scattered without riders. That includes Boo, who is running circles around the arena, almost knocking over the commander, who's trying to chase him down and grab his reins.

I hear shouts and turn to see Smush and Bandit tussling on the ground. Bandit finds an opening and punches Smush across the jaw, but then he lets out a howl and grabs his hand.

Before I know it, I'm charging Bandit. It's like I'm watching from outside my body as I ram him so hard, his helmet goes flying. I don't feel anything, but my head is spinning, and then he's in my face, fire in his eyes, and his fist is the last thing I see.

"Cole, wake up!" I open a eye and see Coach looking down at me. "We need to get you out of here."

She helps me up, and I almost upchuck. I'm still dizzy. "Wait," I say.

"Come, I'll help you. Can you stand?" She gets me to my feet and has a arm around me as we move toward the barn door.

I look over in a haze and see Smush on his knees, arms behind his back, being interrogated by cops. "The cops? What's goin' on?"

"Things got out of hand," she says. "You need to get checked out. I think you have a concussion or something. You had quite a bang to your head. I'll drive you."

She's pulling me away. "But—" I reach out toward Smush, but he don't see me.

We get to the parking lot, and I catch a glimpse of Maverick talking to another cop. And then I see Ruthie behind him, grinding her jaw and looking pissed.

She sees me but doesn't say anything—just watches as I get put into Coach's truck. My head is spinning, and I fall into the passenger seat. "Try to stay awake," Coach says as she gets in. "I'll get you to the ER."

The ride there is a blur, but I kinda remember watching her driving me and thinking: *Why is she here with me instead of with the Generals?*

Maybe something about being knocked out of my senses makes me say: "Can I ask you somethin'?"

She looks at me, concerned. "What?"

I think about what I wanna ask, then clear my throat. "Do you think it'd be good if I went to school here?"

She blinks, taken off guard. Maybe that question makes her even more worried about me having a concussion. "That would depend on why you'd want to come here," she says, like she's just trying to keep me focused.

I close my eyes. "I dunno. To get into college?" I say, holding my head.

"Oh, Cole . . ." she says, putting her hand on my knee. After a long beat, she adds, "I'm so sorry."

Sorry? For what?

My head is hurting from the bumpy drive. I'm

trying real hard to decipher that message. "You don't think I belong? You don't think I'm good enough?"

"I'm saying you're not ready. And that it's not what you need to be thinking about right now."

That's not the answer I wanted. I close my eyes and let the pain take over.

We show up at the ER, where they check me over and take an MRI. I'm getting nervous about how we're gonna pay for all this, but Coach says the Academy has insurance and that I shouldn't worry about it.

Turns out I have a mild concussion along with some scrapes and bruises. They say I'll live.

"Must be that hard head of yours," says Coach.

She calls Harp, of course. He comes down, but he don't say a word in front of her until she mentions Smush. Then his eyes start burning and he cusses to himself. "I should've known," he mutters.

They both stay for a few hours until I get cleared to go. "We'll reevaluate after you take a few days off" is all I remember Coach saying to me.

Harp drives me home in silence. I just sit there, letting everything sink in. *What was I thinking?* I musta embarrassed everyone—Coach, Ruthie, the commander. Even Ronnie's probably taking down all the pics with me and Smush in them.

The doc said it was okay for me to sleep, so Harp gives me a painkiller and puts me straight to bed. "We'll talk about this tomorrow," he says flatly. But I can see he's angry and upset *and* feeling sorry for me all at the same time.

It don't feel good to be a disappointment to everyone at once. I close my eyes and watch the stars in my head. Now what?

TWENTY-FOUR

Ever wake up from a bad dream that felt like your life had been ruined, only to realize it was just a dream and everything's cool now? That's how I feel when I open my eyes. I don't know how long I've been asleep, but it feels like forever.

But when I roll over, my head reminds me it was all real: The clinic. The kiss. The game. The fall. The fight. The hospital. I start coughing, and every cough feels like an explosion in my head.

Dang. It wasn't a dream.

Trying to sit up feels like I'm a hundred years old. I dangle my feet over the side and stare at them for the longest time. Then it hits me.

I blew it.

Yesterday I thought somewhere in the back of my head that I could magically impress everyone so much, they'd just invite me to go to the Academy. What was I thinking? That I'd get a free ride? That maybe me and Ruthie would be a thing and she'd help me improve my grades and we'd both take over the Generals next year when Maverick graduates?

The thought of going back to the Academy now and pretending that yesterday never happened seem so far away that it might as well be a dream. I'm pretty sure Coach told Harp I shouldn't come back, that Ruthie's mom told her to stay away from me, and that Smush is just waiting to tell me I'm a cowboy, not some fancy polo player. And the Generals—I'm pretty sure next time they see me, I got a beating coming my way.

I close my eyes again, and all I wanna do is lie back down and go to sleep for another few years, till high school is done. I don't wanna see or talk to anyone about yesterday. Ever.

But that's when I smell . . . *food*?

I slowly get up and follow the smell. It's coming from the hole in the wall that connects my room to Harp's place. I must be dreaming. Harp is serving . . . breakfast.

"Sit," he says.

Bacon. Eggs. Toast. Burnt, runny, and soggy. But it's food. And even if my head hurts, I'm starving.

I do what he says. Then I remember Boo must still be at the Academy. The last thing I wanna do is show my face there to pick up my horse, but I can't just leave him there.

"What about Boo?" I ask.

"He's here. Bob picked him up. You need to eat."

He watches me dig in. Even though chewing makes my head hurt, my stomach speaks even louder. He sits and joins me, and then it hits me: I ain't never sat down and had a meal with Harp before. He seem to read my mind. "Don't get used to it. I just felt like making my son breakfast is all."

I nod. I see he poured me a coffee. I never had coffee, but he's drinking it, so I drink it too. It's sweet and bitter at the same time. I like it.

"I was worried you mighta got kicked in the head, but you look all right. No marks, no blood. Mild concuss ain't gonna kill you."

I see two aspirin near my plate, so I swallow them and chow down. I finish the plate off in, like, thirty seconds. He sits there, watching, then pushes his plate over. "I'm not hungry."

I wait a second to see if he's joking, then grab it to demolish his as well. But suddenly my mind starts wandering to yesterday and all the things that went down, and I push the plate away.

"I don't think I'm goin' back to the Academy," I say.

"Today?" he asks.

"Ever," I say.

I'm waiting for the I-told-you-so about Smush, but instead he nods, studies my face. "I get it," he says.

"Get what?" I ask.

"Hiding is definitely easier." He gets up, like he's done.

Say what?

He sees my look. Laughs. "Look. I get it. Life would be a whole lot easier if we just ducked out and stayed hidden. If I gave up on the barn and let them shut us down last year, woulda been a lot less headaches for me."

"If I remember right, it was me who stood up to them first," I say.

He lets that slide. "And your school. They could make a stink to get seen by the district so they could get you the equipment and books you all deserve, but that would be hard."

I know Ms. Butler sits down for no one. "Principal

is there pushin' every day. She's trying to make things better."

"Uh-huh. And your friend, the one with the . . ." He's gesturing to his face but can't say it.

"Ruthie?"

"Yeah. I'm sure she's tired of everyone staring at her all the time. Would be easier to stay home and sulk over it."

I'm getting his point: the whole get-back-up-on-your-horse thing. Feels old. "What about Smush? His problem is he's out there *too* much."

"Maybe. He could lay low, but seems to me, he wants us to see him as somebody who made something of himself."

I stare at my plate. "I still don't wanna go back. Coach can wait to get that debt repaid. I'll just keep goin' to North and stay with my own."

He grunts. Half like *Good* and half like *You sure about that?*

"Do what you want. I ain't gonna make you," he says.

"I don't know why you made me go there and think I could belong," I say. "Wish I'da just got a job at McDonald's."

He scratches his head. "I liked the coach, and she was willing to take in Boo. And I guess, somewhere in the back of my head, I thought you were tough enough to handle it. The whole thing about you belonging there? That's all you. So you better just get on with it, then." He starts cleaning up.

"With what?" I ask.

He stops and looks at me. "The rest of your life."

TWENTY-FIVE

Smush is waiting for me after school the next day. I look around to make sure Harp ain't anywhere to be seen, then get into his ride.

We sit there for a minute, watching students head home. "Are you gonna tell me what happened, or what?" I ask finally. "Did they arrest you?"

He looks at me like I should know all this. "I stood up for you, man. What else?" He seems a little pissed. "And, no, they didn't arrest me, 'cause I threatened to sue them."

I almost felt sorry for him for a minute, but right now he's kinda ticking me off.

"I'm doin' fine, by the way," I say. "Only a concussion. Oh, and I lost my job 'cause a you."

He looks ahead, says nothing, but I can tell he feels bad. "I may have acted outta turn."

"Ya think?"

He looks at me. "I ain't sorry. I saw what he did to you. Family gotta stand up for each other." But then he seems like maybe he does regret it. He reaches into his pocket.

"I got something for you."

He drops a stack of bills into my lap.

"What's this?" I ask.

"Whatchou call it, workman's comp. You know, 'cause you got hurt at work."

I blink. I ain't touched that much cash before.

"I can't take this," I say.

"You have to. That's for . . . me messin' up your situation. Consider it an investment."

"In what?" I ask.

"In you, fool."

"You gonna lose your money."

He looks at me. "You'll find your way. Invest it. Like me."

"Invest it?" I say. "The only thing you ever invested in is—" I don't wanna say it, but he knows.

He grunts. Then he reaches into the back seat, pulls out a folder, and hands it to me. "Check this out."

"What's this?" I thumb through a stack of papers. Real-estate offerings. Condos. Businesses. Houses. "You gonna buy a house?"

"More than one. And you could join in."

"I got a house."

"Not to live in, fool. To flip," he says.

"'Flip'? Man, the only thing I'll be flippin' is burgers," I say.

He sits back, watches more students leaving school. "I never graduated, ya know?"

"Yeah, I know," I say.

"But most of them won't be better off than me," he says. "And I'm thinkin' ahead. Plannin' my future. I'm not gonna be in my current business forever. I gotta raise capital. But then I take that capital and invest it, see? I buy a property low, before 'hoods is gentrified. Then I fix up these dumps and flip 'em to these white, yoga-lovin', mocha latte-drinkin' suckers."

I laugh. "So, you like a real-estate mogul now?" I think about how maybe he could flip Mama one of these houses to help her move here. Then I say, "Maybe you can buy the Ritz and make it ours once and for all."

He shakes his head. "City owns that building. They

waitin' for the right time to flip it themselves. Just a matter of time. The lot across the street is gonna be bought up by a developer, and they'll have a foothold. That's how it works. Plant a flag, then the rest come runnin'."

I stare at my shoes. "You know that for a fact?"

He nods. "Someone will close a deal with the city in the next year or so. In the long run, there's no point in stayin'. You gotta think your way outta here, cuz. Otherwise, you won't never leave."

"Maybe I don't wanna leave," I say.

He breathes out real slow like, then leans over and grabs me by the collar. *Tight.* He pulls me in close. "Listen to me good, cuz. The horse thing is cool for now, but you? You're not stayin' here. Find a way to make some scratch. Invest in your future. Go to college or make a business. Then get out."

I'm having a hard time breathing, and he sees it, so he lets go. "I thought you said I belonged here."

Then he starts his car and drives me back. Doesn't say another thing.

TWENTY-SIX

It feels weird not going to work at the Academy. I feel bad about letting Coach down—so bad, I don't even return her call. But every time I think about going over there, I think about Ruthie. She didn't text me after it all went down, and I can't imagine what she think of me now.

After a couple days, I spotted her starting to text me, but each time, I guess she changed her mind, 'cause she didn't hit send. I kept waiting for something, but nothing came.

Over the next few days, things go back to "normal"—well, how they shoulda been to begin with. I still get up early to take care of Boo, but I have a hard time focusing at school. I keep thinking about polo. Why? What do I care? I should forget it all and get on with it, like Harp said. Go back to the original plan. Forget the Academy.

Classes seem all right. Ms. Butler has made sure we all have desks now. She moved some students around, so classes ain't overflowing, neither. Still not enough textbooks, but we share the few we got. She says things will get better.

Maybe she knows I'm feeling mixed up, 'cause two days in a row she says to me, "You're the change. I believe in you." I don't know what she mean by that, but it does make me feel better about being at North. Now, if only we had what the Academy had, then we could be something.

In world history, Mr. Holland assigns me a paper about world history through sports. He knows I got a horse, so he suggests maybe something with horses. I find myself looking up polo and am surprised by how old it is. It started in Asia way back in ancient times, when it was a training game for guards and soldiers, who played it with up to a hundred men on a team, like it was a actual battle. Now I think I understand where the Generals' attitudes come from.

After school, I'm back home at the Ritz. Boo seems happier to have me around more. We race, ride, mosey around in the park. But I can't get the Academy out of my head, and one time, outta curiosity, I take the bus over and sneak around back just to see what's going on over at the arena. I see a new guy washing down a couple ponies outside the barn. I see Brick walk by, and they exchange a laugh.

Then I see someone with the #3 jersey on: Ruthie. She stops and says something to Brick, who *laughs*.

It feels like she's gone over to the other side. I don't know what to do, so I turn and just walk away.

One day, I'm brushing Boo outside the Ritz when Lil' C-Jay and P'nut show up on their bikes, wanting to play cowboy polo.

"Where's your girlfriend?" asks C-Jay, but he can tell I'm not in any mood.

"None a your business," I say.

"Can we play, anyway?" asks P'nut. I look over and see our makeshift goals is still sitting on the fields, so I say, "Go for it. But I got no gear for you."

"That's okay. We'll make our own."

They ride home and return with a few more kids and with peewee football gear and assorted stuff

182

duct-taped together. One kid's got a baseball helmet, catcher's protection, and a bat. Another has a old tennis racket taped to a broom handle—one even got a hockey stick. Finally, someone's sister donates her rubber kickball.

They're in business.

They play on their bikes, zooming around like it's NASCAR, knocking each other off and hitting their helmets with the rackets. It's not like a real match, but it looks kinda fun. Lil' C-Jay shows me videos of other kinds of made-up polo he found online: camel polo, canoe polo, elephant polo, golf-cart polo, snowshoe polo, even Segway polo.

They push me to join in, so I grab a push broom and show them a few moves that Ruthie taught me—teach 'em how it's done. I show 'em how to swing, forehand and backhand. I show them the line of the ball, how to ride off. They bump and grind, then hit the dirt and laugh it off.

We having a good old time. Even if what Smush says about the lot being sold is real, it's good to see it being used for now. I haven't seen any signs go up or developers looking, so maybe he's just blowing hot air. But if he's right, I can't help but think: What's gonna happen to the horses? Where they gonna run? And if the lot goes, is the Ritz next?

The next day, the kids show up again. They try to get Harp to play, but he ain't having it. The fellas start watching 'cause there's no other action going on.

After a week of this, P'nut says, "We wanna play on horses!"

"In polo, they call 'em ponies," I say.

"Yeah, but this cowboy polo!" Lil' C-Jay says.

Only Boo and Lightning is trained, but not enough for a match. Maybe I can show them on Boo how to do it, like my own little clinic. But we need better sticks.

Maybe even a wood horse to practice on. I ask Tex to help me fashion a mallet from a old broom and a piece of one-by-four. If they wanna learn, they gotta start right.

I get a couple crates out and have 'em stand on top and take practice shots. The next day, we strap a old saddle onto a couple sawhorses and have 'em straddle that.

Then I have 'em playing on foot, dribbling and sweeping, like Ruthie taught me.

I don't know why, but I like teaching them. It gives me focus, like there's something to do. But it makes me keep thinking of Ruthie. I wanna text her, but every time I try, I put down the phone again. Not sure why. Instead, I take a picture of some of the kids practicing and text that.

She sends back a happy-face emoji.

I try talking the fellas into letting me get the other horses used to mallets and balls. At first, they say no. They don't like the idea of their horses playing polo. "It ain't cowboy," Bob says.

One day, Tex pulls up in his truck. "Lookee what I found."

In the back of his pickup is a old set of croquet mallets. "You found those? Who be playin' this around here?"

"And they're short enough for your shorties there." When I tell him soon they'll be up on horseback, he thinks and comes back later with a pile of old broom handles and strips of leather. Spends the afternoon showing the kids how to make their own mallets. He shaves the croquet heads down, fashions them with sticks, makes handles by wrapping them with leather.

Mallets.

The next day, he's there with old volleyball kneepads and elbow pads and shin guards from soccer. "What'd you do—rob a sportin' goods store?" I ask. "Musta fell offa truck," he says.

The next day, it's a bunch of beat-up hockey helmets with face guards. Everything is old and worn, like what you might see at a thrift store or run-down high school. The kids love it. They scrap and somehow don't get hurt. Even on bikes. The girls might even be a little tougher than the boys.

But they still wanna play on horses.

I work on Bob first. "You know Harp makes fun of you 'cause you wouldn't last a second playin' polo against him, right?"

"Is that right?" He don't believe me, which makes sense, since I made it up.

"Yeah. At least let me teach your horse what's up." I think he likes seeing me motivated, so he says, "Knock yourself out."

The fellas think it's funny at first, making Jamaica Bob carry a mallet every time he's around his horse, Marley. But that's how you get horses used to it. And that red kickball too. I put it in the water trough, or sometimes in his stall. At first, horses are afraid of things they don't know, but once they get used to them, they like to play. Soon I get Marley and Lightning and Boo chasing that ball around the field.

One day, me and the kids is playing on bikes and on foot and I decide to bring out the horses to see what happens. I get up on Boo, C-Jay gets up on Marley, since Bob still don't wanna play, and the guys hoot and holler. It's all in fun. Harp isn't around, but Lightning wants in too.

"Need a hand, cuz?"

Smush.

The guys are wary of him, but still fist-bumps and nods happen. "You lucky Harp's not here," I say.

"Good. Then let's play."

I eye him. "Last time wasn't so good."

"That's 'cause I wasn't in the game. I been practicing."

"'Practicing'? How?" I ask.

"I been playin' in my mind. Without the ball or pony," he says, like he's a Jedi or something.

"Seriously. Why you wanna play this? It's stupid. We just messin' around," I say.

"I ain't gonna ruin it for you, cuz. I'm gonna be good—you'll see. I wanna help out with the kids, ya know?"

He gets Lightning and starts saddling him. C-Jay looks at me, eyebrows raised.

I know if Harp finds out, I'll never hear the end of it.

"We only have three horses, and they all wanna play," I say, pointing to the kids.

He shrugs. "Well, we gotta show them how it's done. You know, old school. When they ready, they'll get their chance."

I don't like it, but he's not waiting for my approval. He grabs a mallet and gets up on Lightning. "Maybe you wanna start with a little one-on-one demo?"

So we do. C-Jay sits out, and you know what? We have fun, me an' him, going at it street ball–style, the kids cheering us on. Boo and Lightning seem to be into it. The field is a bit uneven, but the big red kickball bounces around over anything and gets where it needs to. I score the first goal.

Boom. "Watch and learn," I say to Smush.

Cuz is never one to back down. He takes the ball and somehow gets Lightning to do a fake-out Shake n' Bake basketball move and scores on me. "Told you I been practicing. I thought you said you wuz good?"

It's on. Some of the kids wanna join in, so they hop on their bikes and ride around the perimeter, knocking the ball back into play when it goes sailing outta bounds. One of the dogs is let loose and is running in between. It's like a three-ring circus. I notice the fellas making side bets, and I do my own inventing, a kind of crossover dribble that leaves Smush in the dust. When I hit eleven first, I call it.

"That's a match, sucker."

Smush shakes his head. "You got lucky, cuz. I just walked in off the streets, but give me some time, and you'll be on the run."

We take a break. The sun is setting. The lights come on. The crackle of a gunshot in the near distance goes ignored. Dogs bark. Cats laze about. We sit under the tent and shoot the breeze.

"Man, we should take this show on the road. People will pay good money to see this," says Smush. "It's like a mash-up polo: part cowboy, part b-ball, all street."

"You crazy, man. This is a free-for-all."

He's looking through the pile of mismatched protective gear.

"Forget cowboy polo. You'd be wearing cowboy hats and boots and stuff like that. This is beyond that— it's like *black* cowboy polo but with some *Mad Max: Fury Road* action. We should get some of them dope costumes and do it up—then you got a show. You just need to trick this gear out some more."

He grabs a beat-up helmet and shoulder pads. "Hold up." He rummages through his backpack. Takes out some spray cans. Goes to work on my gear, painting lightning bolts and crazy images on it. Drapes a old mop head around my neck. Takes a push broom head, grabs Tex's drill, and drills it to the top on my helmet like a crazy flattop!

I put it all on, and everyone stands back and nods. "Looks more like Black Panther," I say. "Wakanda!"

Smush grins and reaches into his pocket and pulls out his sunglasses. He puts them on me. "Now you talkin'," he says.

I cross my arms and take my badass pose. "What happens in black cowboy polo *stays* in black cowboy polo."

"I sure hope so. I leave you alone for few weeks, and now you're doing Halloween costumes?"

I turn around and see Ruthie on her bike with a few mallets over her shoulder. I kind of stand there, jaw open, my mind blank. "So this is your version of cowboy polo now?" she asks. She tilts her head, considering my outfit. "Maybe you want to teach *me* how to play?"

TWENTY-SEVEN

I don't ask what she's doing here. I'm just happy to see her again. But she offers sheepishly, "I just wanted to see what you were up to."

There's so much I wanna tell her—my mind races, but somehow nothing comes out. She gets it. "Good. So, are we doing this, or what?"

"You can use my horse," says Bob.

"I want one of those outfits, though," she adds.

Smush grins in approval. "I knew you had good taste."

She turns and trains her gaze on Smush. "But first, before we do anything, what do you have to say for yourself?"

His smile disappears. He knows he has a lot to answer for about what went down at the clinic. "My bad."

"Your *bad*?"

He shrugs. "Look, I know I messed up. I know that. You reached out with good intentions and stuff, and I messed it all up for you and yours. I'm sorry. Really. It won't happen again."

Wow. He didn't even say that to me.

He holds out his hand to her. She looks at it and hugs him instead. "Game on," she says.

An hour later, all three of us are tricked out: She's got a flaming-red brush head coming off her helmet, with flames on her pads and shin guards. Smush got lions and Africa all over his and has fashioned a horn coming out his helmet.

I tell her we don't really have rules, and that it's kind of every man for himself, and we play to eleven and no fouls, and if you fall off, you can play on foot or jump on a bike, and she's making faces throughout. "That's not polo," she says.

"Now you got it," says Smush. "It's black cowboy

polo. And we ain't usin' your fancy sticks." He tosses her a homemade mallet that one of the kids put together.

She laughs. It's good to see her laugh again. I wanna ask her about everything. About that day. About how it is playing with Maverick and them. About our kiss. But that can all wait. Right now, it's game time.

The sun is low in the sky. Long shadows cover the lot. But there's still enough light to play one match.

But even playing cowboy-style, it's clear she's the one with game. On Marley, she runs rings around us. Twice, she almost knocks Smush off, like some kinda payback for his ruining the clinic. He knows it and takes it. And in the end, the score says it all.

It's 11–6–2. I got the 6, Smush 2. And unfortunately for me, C-Jay recorded it on his phone and puts it up on YouTube.

"I got a following, ya know? I been puttin' up cowboy polo videos for a few weeks now," C-Jay says.

"How many followers you got?" I ask, worried.

He thinks. "Like maybe forty?"

I can live with forty.

"You're getting better," Ruthie says when she rides up to me. "You just need a good coach is all."

"Oh, yeah?" I say. "You got any recommendations?"

She takes off her helmet, looks around.

"I might have some free time."

"Really? What about the Academy?"

She shrugs. "It's all right. I'm like the misfit of George Washington. Since Bandit's sidelined with his broken hand, not a day goes by when they don't remind me that I'm no Bandit. They don't like my style and don't like playing with a girl. Especially if she's a freak. But at least I'm in the game now."

"Yeah, I don't know that I could do that," I say. She looks at me, not sure if that's a dig or not. It's not.

"You can always join our team," Smush says.

I laugh. "We might not be the Generals, but we got grit. I'm thinkin' we should call ourselves . . . the *Misfits*."

"That about right," says Smush.

Ruthie considers it. "Hmm, I don't know. What's it pay?"

Pay? "Tex says riches come from livin' life to the fullest," I offer.

"So, nothing?" She ponders that. "I'll consider it . . ."

We both smiling. Until—

Jamaica Bob hustles up outta the dark. "Yo, Smush. Harp's coming. You better git."

Smush looks over as Bob takes Lightning's reins.

"Good. I wanna talk to him," he says, sliding off the horse.

"Son, I don't think that's a good idea. Maybe give it some time. Like six months or so."

Smush takes off his helmet and pads. "Nah, he always talkin' about manning up, taking responsibility. I ain't afraid . . ."

Me and Ruthie watch as he heads toward Harper's truck as it pulls up. "I don't like where this is goin'," I say.

Harp sees Smush and gets outta his truck. I can see them exchanging words, and they don't look like nice ones.

I head over on Boo. Harp is laying into Smush when I get there. "You're not welcome here anymore, Smush."

"I said I was sorry, Harp. I was just protectin' your boy," he says. But he don't sound sorry.

"Your way of life—it's not how we do things here," Harp snaps.

"I was tryin' to help," Smush says. "I was trying to—"

"I know you been dealing again. And I know you been getting my boy involved."

"Now, Harp, that's not true. I—"

Harp digs through his pocket and pulls out a wad of cash. My wad, from my room. "Yeah? Then, what's this?" He glares at Smush.

Not again.

"It's not what you think, Harp. He gave that to me," I say.

Now he's glaring at me. "We don't take gifts that come from drug money. We make our money honest."

He holds it out for Smush to take. Smush wants to defend himself, but he know better.

"Whatever, man," Smush says, then looks at me. "Sorry, cuz." He takes the money and shoves it in his pocket. "See you around."

Harp watches him head off into the dark till he disappears. Then he says to me, loud enough for Smush to hear, "I don't want you hanging with Smush anymore."

I can't agree to that. "But he's family."

He shakes his head. "Not no more. And take that stuff off. Playtime's over."

He storms off back home, leaving me and Ruthie and the guys in an awkward moment.

Tex breaks the tension. "I can give you a ride home, miss," he says to Ruthie.

"I'll come too," I say.

"No," she says. "You go home. I seen your dad's look before in my mom, and you'll only make it worse." She takes off her gear and hands me her mallets. "You'll hold on to these for me?"

I nod. "Sure. Come back anytime." And I mean it.

TWENTY-EIGHT

I been laying low for three days. I try to be good without Harp telling me. Get up on time, get myself to school, do homework, take care of Boo. When the kids come by to play cowboy polo, I tell 'em, not now. I even help Harp do repairs around the stables, though I can't saw or hammer straight. But I know what a good tack room looks like, so I make one for the Ritz. That gets a nod outta him.

In between, we don't talk about much. We just do. I know better than to bring up Smush, but every time we driving, I'm looking out for his car. I text him on the sly, but I don't hear nothing back. Ruthie checks in with me, texting me a selfie of her at the Academy, but I got nothing to report back.

Then, one day, I'm in the stable, mucking up after Boo, and I turn and see Harp standing there with the weirdest look on his face. Immediately I know something's up.

"Come with me," he says. His voice is soft, uneven.

We get in the truck and start driving. "Where we goin'?" I ask.

"Smush was shot," he says, matter-of-fact.

"What?" My heart jumps. "Where he at?"

"County."

I'm confused. "Hospital or lockup?"

He looks at me, concern in his eyes, and I realize how messed up that question is.

We park at the hospital. I'm about to jump out, but he puts a hand on my chest. "It's not good."

He holds his hand there, and I know he can feel my heart racing. I refuse to cry. "Let's go," I say. I slide out the truck.

We wander through hallways, trying to find the right nurses' station. Harp asks for Derrick, and it takes me a beat to remember that's Smush's real name. We keep getting told to go to another desk, and finally, when we get to the ER, Harp asks that nurse, and she looks at him funny.

"You family?"

Harp pauses, then nods.

She don't give us a straight answer, just tells us to wait while she gets on the phone and whispers something into the receiver.

It's not a doctor that comes to us, but Leroy, in his cop uniform. Harp sees him and his shoulders slump like any fight left in him just got kicked out.

Right then I know: It's too late. He's gone.

Leroy puts a hand on my shoulder. "I'm sorry," he says. I'm so used to him joking around that for a second I think he's gotta be joking now. But this ain't no joke.

"Can we see him?" I ask, my voice trembling.

He shakes his head. "That's not a good idea."

I look down the hall past him and see a couple dudes dressed in white wheeling a gurney out a room with a body covered with a sheet on it. My heart drops. "Is that *him*?"

Harp puts his arm around me and pulls me in tight so I can't see. We stand there for the longest time, me sobbing like I ain't never done for nobody before.

Later, we collect a plastic bag of his belongings from Leroy. Smush's car is impounded, apparently shot up. No one knows why he was killed, but word is, someone had a beef with him or maybe wanted to rob him. He dealt with too many people to know who.

There's no money or phone in his belongings. But in the bag is an Eagles cap he wore sometimes and the folder of his real-estate listings. I tell Harp about Smush's big plan. "You think he bought anything?" I ask.

He looks at the listings. Shakes his head. "They just pipe dreams probably."

We go to Smush's apartment. Harp has a key for some reason, but the door is unlocked anyway. Someone has been in here. Harp is careful, but it's clear nobody's here anymore. Drawers are opened, things overturned. In a closet, we find a small safe, open and empty.

I take a Sixers jersey he liked to wear. There's nothing else worth having. We stand there in his empty apartment.

"He was a good kid once," Harp says. That surprises me. Not that he was, but that Harper thought so. "He just didn't listen. Thought he could game the system."

"He was just doin' what he could," I say.

Harp sighs. "Maybe. Maybe he thought he could write his own rules. But here's the thing: The system games you. Only thing you can do is learn to play it better."

We get ready to leave, but he stops when he spots a photo taped to the wall. It's a selfie of Smush, his old friend Snapper, Harp, and me, sometime last year after I first arrived. I got attitude, like I don't wanna be there. Harp and Smush are on either side of me. I don't remember that picture being taken or where it's at, but he printed it out and stuck it on his wall like it meant something.

Harp reaches down and pulls it off. I think he's gonna throw it away, but instead he carefully takes the tape off and sticks the picture in his jacket pocket.

Every time I try to text Ruthie, I can't bring myself to write the word *dead*. I try calling, but that's even worse. I hang up after two rings and don't pick up when she calls back. I tell myself I'll tell her tomorrow, that she didn't know him that well, that she wouldn't understand.

I don't tell anyone at school. Nobody knew him or cared. Except Snapper, and I ain't seen him in forever. It's sad. They was best friends. Don't seem right that Snapper didn't have his back.

His parents have no funeral, no party, no RIP T-shirts or memorials where he was shot. It's like they don't wanna acknowledge he even existed. Harp shows up at home one day with a weird-looking silver can, and I know it's Smush. He was cremated, and I know they put you in a can in the end. "Parents didn't want him," Harp says, putting the can on the kitchen table.

But that can don't feel like Smush to me. I ride Boo over to the spot where Leroy said they found him. It's just a random street corner next to a empty lot. I look around, but no one's out. Just an empty street. I look on the ground for signs of him, but all I see is broken glass.

I open my backpack and take out that stupid helmet he made, the one with the horn on it. I hang it on a parking sign and tie it on tight.

Then I write SMUSH WAS HERE on it with a orange marker.

TWENTY-NINE

I get a new job, something to take my mind off a everything—Smush, the Academy, Ruthie, my future. It's in Fairmount Park, working with ponies—two things I know. Unfortunately, it's the stupid pony ride where all they do is take little kids around in circles. My job? Walk the ponies around and make sure the kids don't fall off. At least it's only weekends.

Harp seem happy I got a job on my own, even if the owner rips me off 'cause it's all under the table. But me and Harp is both walking on eggshells these days, so anything to get me outta the house is good.

One day, I'm walking a pony named Brat, who's always nipping at my arm 'cause he don't like to be led. There's a snotty kid crying so hard I think he might throw up, and I'm just looking off into the distance, waiting for my shift to end.

Then I see something that stops me in my tracks: Ruthie, on Patches, trail riding.

Unfortunately, she's with the Generals. And even worse, it's Brick who spots me. "Maverick, it's the traitor!" he says, loud enough for me to hear.

I lower my head, hoping they'll move on. I'm in no mood for a fight. The kid is really wailing now, so I turn away from Ruthie and them and hope they go away.

But I hear hoofs coming, so I stop the pony and try to unhook the kid in case there's trouble. He's having a meltdown, so it takes forever to free him and hand him back to his mom. She gives me a look like it's *my* fault. I'm about to tell her whose fault it is when Ruthie appears next me.

"Don't worry: they won't try anything. Why have you been ignoring my texts?" she says.

I wanna tell her, but nothing comes out except "Why are you all ridin' out in the park? I thought that was against the rules."

That throws her. "Coach gave us permission to go on a trail ride" is all she says before the guys ride up. I'm just standing there like a idiot.

Maverick is first to say something. "So, this is your secret training grounds? Impressive."

"You know, I don't work for you no more, so I don't gotta listen to the stupid things that come outta your mouth," I say. He kind of laughs. But he knows I ain't joking.

"Bandit's got a beef to pick with you," he says, jerking his chin at Bandit, who's glaring. "But more than that, you brought dishonor to yourself."

"What do you know about honor?" I say. "You're all about some code—but what about how you treated me? And how you treat Ruthie is even worse." I glance at her, but she looks away.

"What about her?" says Brick. "She's one of us now."

"I doubt that," I say.

"Talk about honor. Your gangster friend *Mush* ruined my season," says Bandit, holding up his cast. "If I didn't have this on, I'd be paying you and your hoodie pal a visit. But he's either hiding or in prison, so I guess that ain't gonna happen."

My face gets hot. I can feel my fist curling up. I

should just tell them, but I don't wanna give them the satisfaction.

"I can speak for myself, Cole," Ruthie says. She looks at them, but I can see the fight is drained outta her. "Come on, we got to get back before roll call" is all she says before turning away.

Brick laughs. "See? Even your girlfriend isn't impressed by you. You were never one of us, *Train*. You should've stayed with your buddies back in the ghetto, where you belong." He turns and follows Ruthie.

Maverick shakes his head. "What were you thinking, Cole? Spots told us you were trying to get into the Academy? Are you kidding? You aren't Cavalry material—not by a long shot. Not even for charity. You'll never be one of us."

Finally, Bandit is left staring me down. "By the way, I saw your little cowboy polo videos. Real cute. You do realize we're in a different league than you, right? Even with my busted hand, we'd still wipe the floor with you. Face it, that's the only sport you and Mush will ever be good at—a pretend sport you play with little kids."

I can feel my blood boiling. One more *Mush*, and I will let loose on this fool.

But Bandit's laughing at me now. "Look at you,

getting all pissed off. You know what? I was mad as hell at you guys, but *now*? I just feel sorry for you. Look at you. You're pathetic. You and your hoodlum friend."

I'm barely holding it in. There's another mother and kid waiting for a ride. *"Mush!"* Bandit kicks at his pony like he's a sled dog. "Mush!"

My boss is staring me down, and all I can do is glare at Bandit's back and think about how I'm gonna end him. But then I catch Ruthie outta the corner of my eye at the end of the corral. And her look stops me cold.

She looks scared.

And suddenly I realize I can't take their bait. I can't lose it, or I'll lose everything—even her.

Especially her.

I take a deep breath, and I try to think of something else. Anything. I shut my eyes, and I see Smush, playing cowboy polo like a little kid. I see Mama watching me as I race against Harper at the Speedway. I think of Ms. Butler and Coach, all reaching out to me. I think of Harp making me breakfast.

I breathe easy when I hear them leave.

I open my eyes and watch them ride off. Without thinking, I take the little girl from her mom and put her gently on her pony. I can hear the Generals' hoofbeats fade into the distance.

"You ready for your ride, sweetheart?" I ask the little girl. She's smiling, eyes open, ready for an adventure. I buckle her in and stand there, looking at that sweet face of hers—

And suddenly I lose it and start crying.

"What's a matter, mister?" the little girl says.

I wipe my tears and pretend I got something in my eye. I look away, only to see Ruthie up on the ridge, looking back at me.

THIRTY

I spend all day thinking of Smush and his dreams and the last thing he ever said to me. I think about how I been looked down on my whole life, how Chester Ave. been ignored, same as North High. I can hear Mama talking about the future and how hard it will be, and I hate that I let them Generals drive me off. I can't get over the look in Smush's eyes when Harp sent him packing, that he was driven off too.

I wake up in a cold sweat. It's the middle of the night. I was having weird dreams about being trapped by a group of horses surrounding me and closing in tighter and tighter. I was in some kinda heavy armor, and fell down to the ground, and I couldn't fight my way back up. The horses started falling on top of me, and we was getting swallowed whole by the earth when I opened my eyes.

I can't go back to sleep, so I do something I never do at this time of night: I get up, get dressed, and go out to the stable.

It's strange seeing Chester Ave. with nobody on it. The lawn chairs out front is all empty. The cars and SUVs is gone. I peek in the barn. All is quiet. I walk down to Boo's stall, and he's standing in the corner, asleep. Or so I think. Half awake, I start doing my morning routine: do a heat check on his legs and joints to feel for any swelling, make sure his manure is green and smells okay, see that he's got enough hay and water. I can see him watching me, and after a while, he comes over for a nibble of hay.

"Hey, boy, you awake too?" I hold on to his neck and listen to his breathing.

I stand there for the longest time, and Boo does too. Maybe he fell asleep again. I almost fall asleep too, until I glance at the wall, and for a second, I think I see Smush standing there. My heart skips a beat till I realize it's just his tricked-out armor hanging on the stall wall, next to Ruthie's mallets.

I wander over and remember him showing off this getup and how it made me laugh.

Dang. I woulda liked seeing me and him take on the Generals in our homemade gear. I laugh at that image. Knowing Smush, he woulda had his boom box blasting as we marched in.

I remember him saying, "If you gonna do somethin', go all in." It bounces around in my head.

Right then and there, I feel something shift in my gut. A feeling I ain't had since I rose up to help save the stable last year. A feeling of having your own posse and riding into battle. Not giving up. Being seen. Like Ruthie dreams about. Like the Ritz and North aim for. Like Smush wished he coulda been. Seen.

"I'm goin' back," I tell Boo. He looks at me like he don't know what I'm talking about. "For Smush."

I look up Ruthie's mom's name, and after a few more clicks, Ruthie's home address comes up. Boo's hoofbeats echo loudly on the streets when there's no traffic about. The city is asleep, except for the odd person sitting in their window, watching me go by.

Maybe they couldn't sleep. Maybe they getting up to hit that five a.m. shift. It's eerie quiet.

I make my way across Fairmount Park. I ain't never seen it so dark. As soon as I'm away from the city lights, I look up and catch my breath.

The stars. I ain't never seen so many in my life! Usually you see one or two, but here? Dang. It's like swimming in the Milky Way.

My GPS takes me to the Heights. I worry somebody gonna call the cops on me, but then I see the houses are behind walls and so far back from the street that ain't nobody gonna see me.

I find Ruthie's street, and then the map says, *You have reached your destination.*

The house is dark. It's a two-story deal, with a big grass yard and long driveway. "What if this isn't her house?" I ask Boo.

He don't answer. I climb off, thinking he'll be more quiet if I walk him. The driveway is gravel, so he's not too loud. I see a SUV in front of the garage. I'm having doubts until I see a bumper sticker: CHUKKERHEADS HAVE MORE FUN.

This is the place.

I figure her bedroom is in back, so I walk Boo around to the backyard, wondering if her dad got a shotgun. I look up and see three big windows and decide to text her: *Look out your window.*

I wait. And wait.

Then I see a curtain move. Then close again. I wonder if that was her mom and if I should take off.

"Maybe we should go," I say to Boo.

I start back around to the side and almost run right into Ruthie. We both scare each other. She recovers first, and before I can say anything, she grabs me in the tightest hug I ever had. I stand there, awkward, until she whispers, "I heard about Smush. I'm so sorry, Cole. I am so sorry."

She means it. I can feel it in her body. I feel her tears on my neck. I bring my hands up and return the hug. "How'd you find out?"

She don't answer at first, just holds me for the longest time, and I let her. I can smell her. She smells like cinnamon and sleep. She's barefoot and in her PJs.

"My mom saw it on the news, but she didn't want to tell me at first. Then when she did, I didn't know what to do."

She kisses me, soft, and whispers "I'm sorry" so quiet, I almost don't catch it.

"I . . . need to do something. It might sound weird," I whisper in her ear. "It has to do with Maverick and them."

She takes my hand and leads me and Boo away

from the house, behind the garage, where there's another yard.

"It's like four in the morning," she says. But she's not mad.

"I couldn't sleep. Plus, I wanted to see you." I hug her.

She sighs. "You're mad about Smush. And you should be," she says. "But don't waste your time with the Generals. Fighting won't help."

I pull back and look her in the eye. "I don't wanna fight them. I wanna *challenge* them."

She looks at me to make sure I mean what I say. "What, at polo? You can't beat them at their game, Cole."

I nod. "I know. I was thinkin' of challenging them to ours."

She raises her eyebrows. "Cowboy polo?"

I nod again.

She thinks about it. "I don't think they'll go down to Chester Ave. No offense."

"Yeah, probably not." I look at her face for the longest time. "But if they did, would you be on my team?"

She considers it long and serious. "I'm always on your team, Cole. But Bandit broke his hand. How's he going to play?"

"He said he could beat us even with a cast. It's not his shootin' hand."

"He said that?"

I nod.

"Well, then, we'll need another misfit. And not one of those little kids. Someone with . . . gravitas."

I don't know exactly what that means, but I get the gist. "World is full of misfits. I think I know one. A big one."

"All right. I'm in," she says, holding out her hand.

I don't shake. "One other thing—" I lean in and kiss her.

She looks at me, surprised, but then we kiss some more. I look over and see Boo watching. I don't care.

When we pull apart, both our hearts is racing.

"What if we had somewhere we could play on neutral ground?" she says. "Then maybe they'd come."

"But wouldn't they have to sneak their ponies out and, like, go AWOL or something?" I ask.

She thinks about it. "Yeah. But for something like this, I think they'd do it. I mean, a chance for payback, in *secret*?"

I nod. "Yeah, I think you right. But where?"

"I think I know a place . . ."

THIRTY-ONE

The police barn door is locked, so we climb up a wood ladder that leads to the hayloft opening. It's pitch-black inside, but we carefully feel our way in. Suddenly, there's a flurry of wings flying past our faces and out into the night sky. We both dive into the hay but come up laughing.

"Pigeons," I say, trying to act calm.

"You were scared. Admit it," Ruthie says.

"I just tripped over you as you was ducking for your life!" I say, laughing. "Okay, maybe I was a little scared. For a second."

We both stand and dust ourselves off. I look at her. It's dark enough where I don't see her skin, just her outline. I kiss her. Then I stop.

"What?" she says.

I pull her toward the moonlight streaming in through the loft opening. It lights up her features, the dark chestnut brown mixing with an ivory white. "That's better." I kiss her again.

She pushes me back.

"What?"

"I didn't come here for that," she says.

"No?"

She gives me a quick kiss. "No. Follow me."

She pulls away and heads for a ladder, using the light from her phone. Once we get to the ground, she takes my hand and leads me across a dirt floor.

"What're you lookin' for?" I ask.

We walk until we stop. We in the middle of the great big barn, but the light from her phone don't reveal much. "Stay here," she says.

I stand there as she wanders into the darkness. I can hear her shuffling about, moving something. Then I hear a *click* and the sound of a big barn door sliding open.

The moonlight streams in, and the barn comes to life. It's huge and wide open.

"Huh. I remember they used to have a buncha stalls in here," I say. I knew the barn was empty when I came by here the last time, but I didn't realize it had been cleared out. The stalls is all gone now.

"They got rid of those. I heard they were going to use it to store all their maintenance vehicles and stuff."

I'm nodding, looking around.

"You know how big this room is?" she asks.

I shrug. "Left my measuring tape behind."

She gives me a shove. "Big enough for a game of cowboy polo, arena-style."

I laugh. "Yeah, I can see it. We could meet at midnight. Maybe put some torches on the walls in here to light it all up. At the strike of twelve, *Game on!*—then the police storm in and arrest us all for trespassin'."

She makes a face. "Oh—didn't I hear a whole story about how you stormed in here when it was full of police and freed a bunch of horses? Think that guy would be afraid of playing a game in an abandoned old barn?"

I get her point.

Game on.

THIRTY-TWO

For a third, we need someone to counter Brick. That means someone with presence who can put the fear in anyone coming toward our goal. I thought of Harper, but he hasn't been involved in this. Jamaica Bob? Nah, too chill. We need someone intimidating who can also ride—least good enough to scare them off.

It takes a while, but I find Snapper eventually. Harp said he heard he had a job down at the 30th Street Station working for the railroad. So I go down there on Saturday, hang out for a good long while. Then suddenly, there he is, on his lunch break, wolfing down a cheesesteak in front of Subway. He looks leaner than last time I saw him, but I still wouldn't mess with him.

When he sees me coming, he stops mid-chew. He don't seem too happy to see me. Not that he don't like me, but I probably remind him too much of Smush.

He puts his sandwich down, and we dap, then hug longer than I woulda thought he'd do.

"Wassup, little man? You found my secret hideout?"

"Not much of a hideout. Harp told me where you was."

He nods, then waits to find out why I'm there.

"You heard?" I ask. He nods.

I pull my backpack off. "I just came to give you something."

I reach into the main pocket, pull out a small glass vial on a string, and hold it out to him.

He looks at it funny. "I don't do drugs no more."

I forgot what it looked like: powder in a vial. "It ain't drugs. It's Smush."

He's confused, but I'm still holding out my arm, so he takes the vial and holds it up to the light.

"His parents didn't want him," I say. "We're gonna scatter his ashes, but I thought maybe you should have a little of him too. For old times' sake."

He shakes his head. "Bruh, that . . . means a lot. It's not right, but—" He keeps looking at it. "You know we stopped being friends, right?"

I shake my head. "No. You was always a friend to him."

I can see his brain going. He just keep staring at the vial.

"It's a necklace," I say. "People do that sometimes. Keeps their loved ones close."

He nods, then puts it around his neck and holds the vial in his hand. "He's so small now."

I laugh 'cause it's just a tiny part of his ashes, but it's a kinda sad laugh, 'cause it's true. He was once a living, breathing dude, bigger than life. Now he's a vial of ash.

"Hey, Snapper . . . I have this crazy idea," I say.

He glances up at me. "Yeah, you and your crazy ideas. I remember. The last one almost got me arrested when we broke into that barn."

I nod but see a in. "Speakin' of that barn . . . this kinda involves that."

He furrows his brow. "I ain't stealing your damn horse again."

I sit down next to him. "Can I show you something?"

I take out my phone, and I show him three or four videos of Smush and us playing cowboy polo back at the lot. He smiles, laughs, even wipes his eyes a coupla times. When it's over, he says, "Looks like fun."

"It is. But we short now. We need a third."

He stares at me for the longest time until he does the math. Then he busts out laughing. "What? You think *I'm* gonna play cowboy polo?"

"We need someone who can put the fear into the other team."

"Dude, I haven't ridden since that night. And I wasn't good then," he says, laughing.

"They say ridin' a horse is like ridin' a bike—you never forget."

"I don't have a bike neither," he says.

"We'll teach you. You'd be like a goalie. Just make 'em have some doubt about comin' into your territory. You don't need to score or run the field. Just put the scare in them and kick the ball upfield to us."

He's thinking. "Let me ask you something: Do I look like a polo player to you?"

I look him up and down. "No. You're too big. But that's kinda the point. And I think Smush woulda wanted you to take his place."

That gets him.

THIRTY-THREE

So now we have a team. Well, at least we got three people. Snapper's not exactly polo-ready, but 'cause he's a former football player, he knows how to slash, bump, and bash, and he's not afraid of being on Lightning, who's alpha enough to mix it up with any horse. I tell Snapper about mind-melding with your horse, and though he don't quite believe me, I catch him whispering to Lightning, "We're teammates. Look out for me, and I'll look out for you."

I guess Snapper's inexperience makes us even with Bandit and his broken hand. And even though we don't have a stable of polo ponies, we got at least three we can use, which should get us through a match.

"So, how we gonna challenge the Generals?" I ask Ruthie.

"I'll just tell Maverick during practice," she says.

"Nah. Gotta be bigger."

"What, like write a proclamation? Send an evite to a match?" she says.

"Not a match." I snap my fingers. "A duel!"

"I think in the old days, if someone wanted to challenge you to a duel, you had to break their sword," she says. "But our swords belong to the Academy. I don't think they'd like that."

"You know, back in Detroit, when the gangs was at war, poppin' off at each other, they'd post videos frontin' their rivals. You know, showin' off and embarrassin' them online."

A grin slowly comes over her face. "We could wear our war gear?"

I nod. "Damn straight. Know what else? Ms. Butler just got some computers donated to the school with all kind of video-editing stuff on it. She even got a camera."

"Anyone know how to work it?" she asks.

I smile. "Got a little filmmaker I know . . ."

"All right," says Lil' C-Jay. "When I say action, you race toward the camera and whack that ball. But don't hit me, okay?"

Turns out our shorty knows a thing or two about shooting video, since he been recording and editing our practices. And he likes them big Hollywood action flicks, 'specially if they got car chases and explosions. He checks out the gear at school (I sneak him in one afternoon), and he promises he can do all kinds of special FX and whatnot.

"Make us look good," I say, hoping he just keeps it in focus.

Ms. Butler likes that I've taken a interest in the video gear. She's turned that room we cleaned out into a computer lab. "See?" she says. "Unexpected doors sometimes lead to new paths. Develop an interest, and soon you'll be leading others down a new path too."

Maybe. I don't tell her what we're doing except that we're filming the horses. She thinks we're doing a western or something. That might not be too far off: the big showdown.

A week later, I invite Ruthie to meet us at North

after school. She's heard about my school, but never been, 'cause her mom thinks it's too dangerous. But seeing it through Ruthie's eyes, I realize how much work Ms. Butler been putting in while I wasn't paying attention: She got the art students to paint some new murals in the hallways, the janitors been cleaning things up, and someone even planted new trees and flowers she got donated. It'll never be the Academy, but it's ours. Ruthie seems surprised.

"You were expectin' prison or something?" I joke, but her reaction tells me maybe she was.

We get to the lab, and C-Jay has a video up on the screen. He turns the lights out as we sit and says, "Get ready to have your head blown off."

He hits play, and immediately it feels like one of them monster-truck commercials: lots of quick cuts, flipping shots, and cheap video FX. There's crazy music, with us charging the camera in slo-mo, hoofs kicking up dirt, balls smashing wood posts. Every time the ball gets smacked, C-Jay's added an explosion. The music builds, and then it's me and Ruthie, backlit with our Mad Max gear. C-Jay took my voice and made it all deep and added echo to make it sound huge.

"GENERALS! CONSIDER THIS A CHALLENGE. THIS FRIDAY. MIDNIGHT AT THE OLD POLICE

BARN IN THE PARK. THE MISFITS WILL DESTROY YOU. BE THERE, OR BE—" We draw an imaginary square, which Boo kicks, and it explodes! All in thirty seconds.

C-Jay hits the lights, and Ruthie and me stare at the screen. She doesn't say anything for a few seconds. Then a grin comes over her face. "Well, they're not gonna ignore *that*."

I'm not gonna lie: we look badass. "I mean, we're pretty much callin' them chicken if they don't come, right?"

She takes my hand. "We can still get our butts kicked."

I nod. "Yeah. But at least we doin' it our way. And we got a badass video outta it."

C-Jay's grinning. "Can I come?"

I shake my head. "Past your bedtime, shorty. Besides, we don't want any witnesses. We lose, it'll be just us three."

THIRTY-FOUR

At midnight, Fairmount Park is totally empty. The roads and trails are dark, and the forest's pitch-black. And the night of the duel, there's a weird fog hanging over everything. Scary if you didn't know your way around.

When Maverick, Bandit, and Brick show up, the light from the phones they're using to see the path makes them look like ghosts coming out the fog. It's eerie, but we ready for them.

They approach the barn door. "Hold up," says Maverick. He shines his light on the door until it hits our sign: BATTLE AT FAIRMOUNT PARK. All the lights inside is off.

"Is this it?" asks Bandit. "'Battle'—that sounds as stupid as it probably is."

Brick peers into the darkness. He can't see us. "No-shows," he says. "I knew they'd chicken out. What a waste of—"

"Hit it," whispers Ruthie.

I press play on my phone. A local Philly beat tape that Smush turned me onto kicks in loud and heavy, rocking the joint. Their ponies jump, and the boys struggle to settle them down.

"That's not funny!" I hear Brick shout, barely.

"Ready?" I shout to Ruthie. She nods.

I feel like a fool, but, hey—let's do this. She hits the on switch for the floodlight we put on the ground behind us for maximum effect.

"What the—?" says Maverick.

All they can see is our silhouettes, and we look badass if I do say so myself. Like warriors. Misfit warriors. The ponies is wearing armor we made outta old CDs tied together with string, and the floodlights bounce off the discs, shooting explosions of light all around us.

I speak into my phone. My voice-changer app makes me sound like a demon monster. "DO YOU DARE TAKE ON THE MISFITS?" I declare, making their ponies uneasy.

Maverick and Brick look at each other. "What the hell is this?" Bandit yells.

"PREPARE TO MEET YOUR DOOM!" I thunder, and do a maniacal laugh.

"Too much," says Ruthie.

"SORRY," I say, but that thunders across the barn too. I stumble about, finally shut the voice app off, and move forward on Boo. Ruthie rides alongside on Marley. The boys are at a disadvantage, looking straight into the light. They're dressed in their best polo gear, blue pressed shirts, crisp white pants, leather armor, boots and helmets gleaming. They move forward on their best ponies, who look equally sharp—a perfect match.

In comparison, we're looking rough-and-tumble. Our Black Cowboy–Mad Max–Wakanda mash-up gear is played up for maximum effect. Even Boo and Marley got on nontoxic paint, making them look like fierce skeletons—we like the Two-Horse People of the Apocalypse!

We meet in the middle. They still looking into the light, but they can see enough to know we mean business.

"Damn, Spots, at least you guys got style, I'll give you that," says Maverick. "Too bad this isn't Halloween. I thought you'd look like cowboys, at least."

Brick makes a face, shaking his head. "I thought you was one of us," he says.

"I was never one of you, and you make sure I know it every day," she answers.

"Girl, can't you take a joke?" says Bandit. "You think you're the first to be razzed at the Academy? Imagine what we said about Brick here when he first walked in." Brick squirms at the memory.

"Enough—Maverick, we gonna do this, or what?" I say in my own voice.

He gives me a steely look. "There's only two of you. Bandit's still game, even with his cast. Where's your third? Or is this some kinda lame cowboy polo crap?"

"In cowboy polo, there are no rules," I say dramatically. "Anything goes. It's like pickup ball—one-on-one, two-on-two—don't matter. All that matters is what happens in the arena."

Maverick is looking around our space. "I always thought there were too many rules to the game. We like to mix it up—as you and Smush got to find out."

I take a step forward on Boo, but Ruthie cuts me off. Maverick holds up his hands. "Sorry about your friend. That's the only reason we came, really. After we heard, we knew you were challenging us to defend his honor."

"Like he had any," adds Brick.

Maverick slaps him in the arm with his mallet. Brick winces. "We respect that code, even if we didn't respect him. You were with us long enough to earn a chance to defend whatever honor you might have left."

"Which isn't much after your sneak attack on me," says Bandit. "That's not gonna happen again."

I don't know what to say to that. It's not about honor, or even beating them—it's about them knowing we're not gonna just fold and go away. "We don't need rules, but we don't fight dirty neither," I say. "We stand up for what's ours."

"Yeah, and what's that?"

"Respect." I stare at Brick, daring him to say something.

"That's real sweet," says Brick. "But arena ball is always three-on-three, rules or no rules. Otherwise, it's not even a game. So, if you don't have a third—"

"Oh, we got a third, all right." I been waiting for our big reveal. I hit the next song on my playlist and Method Man's "Bring the Pain" comes blasting outta the darkness. Snapper, in his old black football uniform tricked out with gold spray paint and a plastic crown, holds his Bluetooth speaker high as he rides in on Lightning, like a Wakanda warrior ready for battle.

I'm grinning ear to ear. "Old school. Can you dig it?"

"You sure he's ready to play?" Ruthie says to me through gritted teeth.

"We been trainin', and he ain't afraid of messin' up. But it don't matter. Image is everything," I say.

"I hear y'all playing some midnight ball!" Snapper roars. "I'm here to represent!" Seeing him come to life like that has *me* scared.

Brick is panicking. "What the—?"

"He's our number three, Brick."

Snapper rides up in between Ruthie and me, and we all fist-bump. He howls, "I'm ready to do some damage tonight!"

He grooves to the beat for the whole song, punching the air in a imaginary beatdown as he moves out and circles them. I let him do it, 'cause I can see he's getting in the Generals' heads.

The song ends. Snapper grins. "Got a special playlist for the match. You know, to keep things *real.*"

"What is this, 1999?" says Maverick. "Fine, you got a third. By the looks of it, he's probably as good as Smush was, which is to say not at all. You know what they say: the bigger they are, the harder they fall."

I ain't never seen anyone try to put Snapper in his place. I see his muscles tense up, like he's about to go Hulk. "Easy," I say. "Save it for the game."

He looks at me sideways. "No rules, right?"

"No rules . . . except you can't actually kill them, right?"

His face softens. "Who do I look like? I got a baby girl, remember?"

Bandit interrupts. "Doesn't matter to me what you got. You still don't have what it takes to beat us."

Maverick moves toward us. "So how does this 'game' work, then, if there are no rules?"

"Well, there's one rule, the playground rule: first to eleven wins," Ruthie say.

"Eleven? What is this crap?" says Maverick. "How many chukkers?"

"No chukkers. No fouls, no penalty shots. No time limits," says Ruthie.

"Should be quick, then," says Maverick. "Especially since we don't have extra ponies to swap in."

"Could be real quick," Snapper adds, punching his fist.

"Nice try," says Bandit. "You can throw anything at us, and we'll still have more skills than you *misfits*."

"So how 'bout upping the ante, then? Let's make

it interesting," Ruthie says. That gets Maverick's attention. And mine.

"What are you doin'?" I whisper to her.

"Like a bet?" says Maverick.

"A bet . . . but without money," she says. Now I'm kinda worried.

"What, you can't put your money where your mouth is?" asks Brick.

"This'll be better than money," she says. "You win—we all come to work for you at the Academy. You can boss us around all you like. We'll be your little servants."

They seem to like that idea, but I don't. I haven't squared things with Coach. And the idea of being their servants don't sit well neither. "Um—" I raise my hand.

"But if *we* win—" Ruthie adds.

"Fat chance," says Brick.

"If we win," she repeats, "you *all* go work for Cole at the Chester Ave. stables."

Now *that* I like.

"*What?*" says Maverick. "Seriously, I wouldn't go into that neighborhood if you paid me. Besides, you know we can't just leave campus anytime we want."

"You did tonight," I say.

"We snuck out, this *one* time," says Maverick. "Unlike you, we have standards to live by."

"You have weekend leave," she counters. "I say, you spend the next . . . four weekends . . . working for Cole. Consider it a community service."

Maverick is shaking his head. "You can say whatever you like, because *you* winning? That isn't gonna happen. We're a well-oiled machine. You? You're like a ghetto Frankenstein—just used up old parts stuck together."

Snapper don't like that. "That's racist, bruh. And what you know about our neighborhood? We been riding horses since the dawn of time. We're cowboys. We hold our own. Our neighborhood might be poor, but we got family and neighbors who go way back. You'll be more than welcome—especially if you do what Cole says."

"Whatever. Let's just get on with it." Maverick catches sight of the red kickball lying on the dirt. "What's *that*?"

"Cowboy polo ball," I say.

Brick nudges him. "I knew it. This is amateur hour."

"Then you should have no problem," Ruthie says.

"It's on," says Brick.

"I'LL SAY WHEN IT'S ON!" a voice rings out.

We all turn to see Harper standing at the far end of the barn.

Oh, snap.

"Did you invite him?" whispers Ruthie. I shake my head.

He walks into the light, glaring at all of us like he just caught us doing some kinda illegal Fight Club, which, given the way we dressed, it kinda looks like we doing. I can't quite read him, so I just say the first thing that comes to my head: "How'd you find us?"

"Your little shorty knocked on my door, asking if you went to the rumble. When I said I didn't know about any rumble, he showed me your little commercial."

"Who is this, your grandpa?" says Brick. Bad move.

Maverick says it more politely. "We're here settling a private matter, sir. So, respectfully, it's not your business."

"I'm this boy's daddy," says Harp. "So his business is *my* business."

I look at Ruthie like the plug just got pulled.

"Looks like Daddy came to your rescue," says Bandit. "Lucky for you."

"That's probably for the better," says Brick. "Go back home, where you belong, and, out of respect for your gangster cousin, we'll forget this ever happened."

Harp glares at them, then turns to me. But instead of cussing me out and sending me home, he . . . winks.

"Cole can make his own call," say Harp. "I'm here to watch. And make sure things stay above board."

I steal a look at Ruthie and Snapper, who are both surprised. Snapper pulls out the vial around his neck and holds it up for all to see. "Oh, it's on. For Smush!"

"For Smush!" me and Ruthie shout.

THIRTY-FIVE

In the great history of wars and battles, the Midnight Battle of Fairmount Park might not rank up there with Gettysburg or one of them World War Z epics, or even with blowing up the Death Star. But for me, it's the real deal. We gonna leave everything on the battlefield, even if we get our butts kicked. And Harper's there to bear witness. Or at least be there for us.

We huddle up. "We gonna do this old school, North Philly–style," says Snapper. "They may got more talent, more skills, and better upbringing, but we got attitude, street smarts, and maybe a few new moves they ain't seen before, am I right?"

"Right!" me and Ruthie shout.

"Hands in," I say.

We all join hands, and I notice outta the corner of my eye Harp recording us on his phone, like a good sports dad. I let it go and focus on the game. "This one's for Smush. He wouldn't care if we lose tonight just as long as we leave our mark."

"Amen," says Snapper. He kisses Smush's vial around his neck and tucks it into his uniform for safekeeping. "Now, let's do this, 'cause I got an early day tomorrow. Taking my kid to the zoo, first time."

"Aww . . ." says Ruthie.

"Guys, are we playin' or showin' baby pictures?" I say.

Snapper looks at me like he could snap my neck. "Okay," I say. "One picture."

He smiles and shows off his little girl on his phone. "Brianna. Gotta teach her to stand up for herself by example, ya know. I may not know how to play polo, but I didn't want to let you guys down. Now let's go show 'em what we got."

We line up in the middle of the barn for the face-off, Snapper and Brick hanging back to man the goals. The spotlights light the room, but the doors are closed so we don't attract any attention. Harp is holding the ball at the sidelines.

"I'm okay with no rules, except for one: No horses get hurt, period," he says. "You run them too long, I'm calling it. You hurt one, I'm calling it. You get hurt? That's up to you. But the horses stay healthy. Got it?"

We all agree. "All right, then—game on!" He throws the ball into the middle of us, and Maverick gets control. Then Ruthie knocks it away—straight at me. I take it on the chest, soccer-style. It bounces three feet off me, and I accidentally kick it up into the air with my mallet.

While we're all looking up, Ruthie goes wide and heads toward the goal. "Wakanda!" I shout as the ball falls straight to me again. I stand up on my stirrups and head-butt the ball over Maverick and Bandit. Ruthie is on the other side, waiting.

"Wakanda!" she shouts as she takes the ball on the bounce and guides it toward the goal. Brick is coming on from her nearside, but instead of playing the line of the ball straight, she bounces it off the wall—and around Brick, so that it boomerangs back to her. Brick gets turned around, and Ruthie gets the ball again, lines up her shot—but Bandit sneaks up on her and hooks her mallet!

In my helmet, all I can hear is my breathing and the sound of Boo's hoofs as they explode up through my body. Off in the distance, Snapper's mixtape thumps in the background. My heart is beating outta my chest as I charge to Ruthie. It's like watching the match through VR and playing a first-person game— only this one's gonna hurt.

Everything that happens feels like a dream. Maverick and Bandit fly around the arena, driving and conquering. They seem to know where the ball is headed, flashing ahead to every spot to keep it in play. But me and Ruthie, we're connected too, *in the flow*, like Coach says, and when we play our two-person game, it's like no one else is out there. I find her, or she finds me.

She missed that first goal, but we're sending a message. We got game, even if it's a bit funky. On the other end, Snapper may not know much, but he knows how to grind it out from his days on the football field. On their attack, the Generals score, but not without Snapper leaving his mark on Maverick with a sideswipe from his elbow.

With the music and everyone flying about, it's a blur. We score our first goal on a pick-an'-roll setup I showed Ruthie a while back. It's not polo, but in a two-person game, I thought it might work. It's rough, but I get a clean shot and let it fly—and it's like everything stops. The ball sails through the air, just ahead of Brick's outreached mallet—right into the goal!

"Ride on!" I shout, like I just hit a buzzer beater. It's the best thing I've ever felt. I give Brick a look that says: *There's more where that came from.* He shakes his head.

Ruthie points over at me, and I hear a "Waaakkkaaaaandaaaaa!" coming from Snapper. He's grinning ear to ear, arms raised.

"Get over it, Train. It's *one* goal. Big whoop," says Brick. "You're still down three."

Maybe. All I know is we're on the board.

"Let's go, Misfits!" I look over and see Harp cheering us on, and it's a weird sight. It's almost like he's proud or something.

He throws the ball in, and suddenly I feel invincible. I don't know how, but I find the ball and then Ruthie, and we shout back n' forth, communicating: "Play the man, not the ball!" "Tail it!" "Yoyoyo! Over here!" "Slow down. Take half hits!" We start reading the other team, look for openings, and next thing I know, I pick Bandit's pocket, stealing the ball and popping it out to Ruthie—who sneaks in another goal.

Bandit stares daggers at me, but I don't care. He's rubbing his cast, and I know he's got more than a few bruises from the last time he tried to ride me into the boards and Boo got in the spirit and slammed back. Plus, I may have swung and hit his leg instead of the ball.

He gets me back, though, on the next exchange. Maybe I'm too cocky, but I get another shot on goal, and when I swing, his mallet connects with mine and breaks my homemade stick in two! My arm is dead, and Brick laughs and waves his finger. "Not in my house!" he yells.

But then I remember one of Tex's rodeo moves, where he taught me how to hold on to the saddle and hang off the side of the horse. "Rodeo move, Boo." I got no mallet, but the ball is in front of me, and I grab the saddle with both hands and swing down and Boo knows what's up and moves just enough so I can kick it into the goal.

Brick can't believe it. "What is that? You can't kick the ball!" he shouts.

"No rules, remember?" I say. "Besides, you broke my mallet. What am I supposed to do?"

Harp grabs me another one and throws it up to me as I ride by. I can't help it. "This is my mallet!" I sing. "There are many like it, but this one is mine! It's my best friend." I kiss it.

We're down one. Trash-talking is one way into their heads, so the trash starts flying.

I don't know how long we been out there, but I'm starting to get tired, which means Boo is tired too. I can feel the sweat on his neck. But no chukkers means no time out and no swapping horses. If we don't use our time right and start pacing ourselves, Harp will call the match.

I can see the same look on the others, though the Generals seem like they got more in 'em, since their horses are used to it. We need a break, but I'm not sure how to get one.

"Anyone up for a time-out?" I ask after the next goal.

"Time-out? There are no time-outs in cowboy polo, don't you know that?" says Brick. They got more stamina than us, and they know it. "Unless you're ready to quit?"

We keep going, but I can see our ponies are slowing down and need a break. The idea of swallowing my pride and calling it for the ponies don't sit well with me.

Then I see Snapper looking up at the barn rafters at something. "Are those . . . bats?"

I look up and see what looks like hundreds of winged rats hanging off the rafters. "Holy—"

Then I get an idea.

I look for the right time and wait till I get a high bounce, free and clear. Then I smack the ball as hard as I can—straight up. It flies into the rafters and—

Snapper's eyes go wide as a flurry of bats descends into the barn, flying every which way! "Run for it!" yells Brick. He and the Generals wave their sticks in the air and make for the barn door. Ruthie and Snapper are ducking low, right behind them. I jump down and start pulling Boo away, but for some reason, Boo isn't freaked—he just watches the bats like a cat chasing a laser light.

I run into Harp as soon as we're out. He seem calm as Dracula, like he gets what I've done. "Not very sportsmanlike," he says.

"Any means necessary," I say, exhausted.

"I don't think that's what Malcolm meant," he says.

"I know you don't mind if the horses get rest. It's like baseball when they call a rain delay, right? This is a bat delay."

He shakes his head, and we watch the bats fly around in a beautiful symmetry. Boo gets his rest on.

"I thought bats were supposed to be nocturnal?" Maverick asks.

"Maybe they're sleeping in," Ruthie suggests, like a smart-ass.

I don't care why they're there. I'm just happy to catch my breath.

It takes a good twenty minutes before the bats completely disappear into the woods and the others agree to go back in.

"Try that again, and you forfeit. Got it?" says Brick. I can see he's shaken 'cause he keeps looking up at the rafters to make sure the bats are gone and won't turn him into a vampire.

I think Bandit almost admires my tactics, even as he calls me a cheater. "Nice try, homie. But even Batman can't rescue you now."

The match resumes, at 8–5, Generals. We take advantage of Brick's distracted head and score two more, back-to-back, where I get to use my Shake n' Bake crossover move. Even Snapper hits a ridiculous pass that flies across the entire pitch and happens to land right in front of Ruthie, who knocks it in. But then the Generals settle and decide we aren't gonna walk outta there winners.

"They mad now," says Snapper.

A minute later, I take a ball to the face, Ruthie gets a seriously bruised arm, and Snapper takes a tumble when he dives for a ball, soccer-style. Two goals are scored—and not by us.

"Looks like game point, punk," says Brick.

We huddle. "We got anything left to throw at them?" Ruthie asks.

"I say we all play offense. They gonna score anyways. Let's throw Snapper up there and see what happens," I say.

"Like a blitz?" he asks.

I nod. "Throw some screens, charge 'em like you crazy. We're not gonna let them win easy."

We join hands. No more Wakanda. "*Misfits* on three."

"One—two—three! Misfits!"

The last few minutes are all fuzzy in my head, but Harper got it all on camera. We played hard, charged 'em, mixed it up North Philly–style. We got in their faces and in their heads. Everyone got beat up—mallets, balls, elbows went flying. More than one black eye and busted lip happened. Even Snapper got a accidental goal, when the ball bounced offa his back, his first and most likely only score.

But at the final throw-in, I was a beat too slow, and Bandit got the ball from me and tore downfield to the goal. Ruthie and Snapper collapsed on him, but he had a move of his own, faking a nearside forehand but leaving it behind for Maverick to pick it up in his wake. Nothing was gonna stop the lieutenant as he exploded toward the goal. I gave chase, but when he let it fly, we knew we was done. I just watched it sail into the goal.

Game.

I expected cheers and more than a few jabs at my ego. But a funny thing happened. We was all so beat-up and exhausted and dazed that we all just sputtered out.

Maverick and Brick high-fived, but it was an effort. More like a realization that they'd escaped humiliation. Harp clapped and pointed my way. That was victory enough.

"Well, we tried," Ruthie says, downcast.

I take her hand. "More than tried. We *showed* 'em."

"Bruh, I'm retired," Snapper says, taking off his helmet. "I'm too old for this. But it was kind of fun." He pauses, then takes the vial off his neck and holds it out to me.

"What am I supposed to do with this?" I say.

He shrugs. "Remember your cuz. The fact that he wanted to play with you shows you how much he looked up to you."

"Looked up to me?" I say, like he's crazy.

He nods. "You don't get it. He may have been older, but he did look up to you. Wished he *was* you, even. The way you stand up for things, the way you keep it on the straight and narrow, keep it 100 . . . that's something to be proud of, even when you lose. *Especially* when you lose." He holds out his fist. I hold out mine.

"Forget Wakanda. Chester Avenue *forever*," he says.

Maverick comes up to us as we're letting the ponies get their drink on. They tired too, but not more than after race day at the Speedway. It's two in the a.m., and I'm ready to collapse, but I've been waiting for Maverick to lay it on thick.

"I expect to see you all bright and early tomorrow," he says, but there's no nastiness in his voice. He holds out his hand. "You done the Misfits proud, Train." For the first time, it feels like he looking at me as a person, not someone to look down on. Maybe I see him the same way too.

I shake his hand. "I'll be there."

"*We'll* be there," says Ruthie.

Maverick looks at Snapper and says, "I get the feeling you were roped into this last minute, so I'm not gonna hold you to it."

Snapper shakes his head. "Well, I did promise my kid I'd take her to zoo, but—"

"But, nothing," Maverick says. "I think your kid is more important than mucking stalls. Don't you think, Train?"

I nod. "If it's okay with you, it's okay with me." I look Snapper in the eyes. "I do feel kinda bad I pulled you into this."

"You didn't make me do nothing, Cole. I came on my own. I guess I'll take y'all up on skipping the work crew because I did promise my daughter. But I'll tell you what—it felt good playing. Or whatever that was. I didn't mind helping you show these boys up." He winks at Maverick, who takes it.

"Thanks," I say. I can't get over that he's here, that he even turned up for my stupid game.

He puts his hand on my shoulder. "No worries. We left it all on the field." He studies the bruise and cut on my face. "Maybe you more than me, cuz."

I like him calling me that.

THIRTY-SIX

Saturday morning. Back at the Academy. I walk into the stables, and Coach is standing there, waiting for me. "Cole."

"Coach," I say.

She notices my face. "Seems like you aren't the only one who had an accident last night."

I look past her and see Maverick, Brick, Bandit, and Ruthie in her office, looking the worse for wear. "They in trouble?"

"Oh, yeah. Rules were broken, procedures ignored, curfews violated, ponies taken off campus. Demotions will be forthcoming," she says.

"Maverick ain't gonna be first lieutenant no more?" I ask. At one time I woulda grinned at that. Not today.

She rolls her eyes. "Don't worry about him. What about you? You here to work?"

"Yes, ma'am."

"Then get to it. A deal's a deal, at least for the moment."

She knows.

Coach turns and walks back to her office. Maverick looks chastened, until I catch his eye and he acts out giving me a black eye with his elbow. He smiles, then points at his own eye. I got him good too.

We're brushing the ponies from last night. Somehow they managed to survive in good shape. I give 'em extra attention, feeling their legs for heat or swelling to make sure they're okay.

After their grilling from Coach, the others join me in the stalls. Somehow it seems like we're on the same playing field now. We're all misfits, and I'm okay with that.

"You lose a rank?" I ask Maverick.

He nods. "Took my sword. Temporary suspension of rank. At least for this month."

Ruthie laughs. "Not so bad down here in the muck, eh, cadet?"

"Say it while you can, plebe," he says. "I just hope she doesn't kick us off the team."

"She won't," says Brick. "They need us, right?"

Everyone nods. "Even if they temporarily suspend us, at least Ruthie will hold down the fort," says Maverick. "She didn't have a curfew to skip out on."

"Maybe next time, I will," she says. "Mom is talking about me becoming a boarder next year."

"Wait—they're going to let *girls* into the dorms now?" Maverick says.

Ruthie gives him the eye. "You got a problem with that?"

He goes back to shoveling. "No. It's just taken long enough. Maybe now we'll have someone to ask to the dance."

She sidles up to me. "Sorry, Mav, I'm taken." She leans over and kisses me on the cheek.

"Dude, I just threw up in my mouth," says Brick. "Don't do that in front of me. It's gross."

"Cole!"

I look back, and Coach waves me over. Bandit shakes his head. "Your turn, dude. Watch out: she's not in a good mood."

"I don't even go to this school," I say, heading over toward Coach's office. She holds the door open for me.

I sit on a crate across from her desk. "I just got off the phone with Harp," she says.

I see her cell phone on her desk. A video is uploaded to it.

"Have you seen this?" she asks, pressing play.

It's the match from last night. I can hear Harp making comments, narrating the action and getting on my case.

"Is he in trouble too?" I ask.

She sidesteps the question. "So whose idea was this in the first place?" she asks.

I cop to it. "Mine."

"*You* invented all this. The costumes. The game?"

"Well . . . me and Ruthie," I say. "And a buncha kids from the neighborhood over on Chester Avenue. And my cousin Smush." Suddenly, my voices catches and I have to turn away for a second. I glance over out the window and see the others glued to our meeting.

I tell her the story. All of it. Including Smush dying.

Afterward, she sits back, thinking. She can't exactly punish me, since I'm not a student, but . . .

She slaps her hand down on the desk. "I think it's time."

I'm thrown. "For . . . ?"

"For me to sponsor your application."

Now I'm really confused. "What application?"

She leans forward, looks me in the eye. "For you to join the Academy. How else are you going to play for us?"

I give her a long hard look. This gotta be a prank. "I don't think Harp can afford—"

She waves me off. "We have a polo scholarship— didn't you know that?"

I nod my head. "I just didn't think . . ."

"It's true, we haven't used it for the past few years, since we don't get many people of color—" She catches herself, rethinks: "Since we don't get many students who don't fit our traditional profile."

"Are you sayin' . . . you'd *pay* for me to come here?" I ask.

"No," she says, laughing. "Not me. The school sponsors—they'd cover you. Might start you as a part of the new day programming, where kids will attend next year like they do a regular high school."

This is almost too much to process. "Do I . . . gotta wear the uniforms?" I ask for some reason.

She laughs. "You mean, the cadet uniforms?" she asks. "Oh, no, I don't think that's for you. You'd wear a school uniform. And of course, the polo gear . . ."

Questions shoot around my head, like: *Why would*

I come here? Am I good enough? Would I even like it?

On the other hand, they do got horses. And then there's Ruthie . . .

I think about Coach's offer for weeks. But one day, Ms. Butler corners me and asks me to help her clear out the old library. The room hasn't been a library for a while, but she got a grant to help her reopen it as a actual place for books again. And it's while we're moving out old desks and chairs and junk with some other volunteers that we get to talking and I tell her about the offer to the Academy. She's surprised and a bit taken aback, but she seem happy for me, even when I tell her I have my doubts.

"Whenever I have trouble deciding something," she says, "I always ask myself: What is the first thing that pops into my head when I'm trying to think of a solution to this problem?"

So I ask myself that, and my answer surprises both me and her: "What if North started their own polo team?"

That seems like a crazy idea, but after I brainstorm more with Ms. Butler, I go and tell Ruthie. She doesn't think I'm stupid and even tells her mom about it. We end up talking to Coach, and it's like a light bulb went off in all our heads.

Tex taught me one thing: when a woman gets an idea in her head, get out the way and let 'em do it. Between Ms. Butler, Ruthie and her mom, and Coach, ideas are hatched, fundraising explored, and 'cause there's no barn at school, locations scouted.

I put off my decision about the Academy and instead start talking up the idea with students at North. People look at me weird, but I don't care. I feel like one of Ms. Butler's unexpected doors has opened . . . and I'm not sure I want to close it.

EPILOGUE

Man, what a motley group!" says Maverick when me and the still-growing North squad show up at the Academy. It's Community Polo Day again, and this time, Ruthie's mom put it together to help out North's polo program *and* make the Academy look good. She's somehow convinced the city councilman in charge of parks to come too, since she's got her eyes on the police barn in the park as a new home base for our team.

"Holy crap, what are you wearing?" asks Brick when he sees our new team shirts.

"Good to see you too." I show off our gear—not a polo shirt, but a T, 'cause that's how we roll. On the front is our names: MISFITS. I spin around and show off the back, where it says RIDE LIKE A CHUKKERHEAD.

"Cute," says Bandit. "But I think you misspelled *knucklehead . . .*"

"Well, *I* think it's cute," says Ruthie, and she comes up on me and kisses me on the cheek.

"Dudes, get a room," says Brick, pretending to have the heaves.

"Just think, you can experience this every day when you come to the Academy," Ruthie says to me. She knows I've put that decision off for the time being, but she likes to say it to get a rise out of Brick and them.

"Maybe I'll wait till the Misfits beat you all first," I say.

"Then I got nothing to worry about, because it'll be a long-ass wait, Train," says Brick.

"Let's get the show on the road!" yells Harp from the stands. The whole gang is here for support: Tex, Jamaica Bob, C-Jay and his friends, Leroy and Snapper and Ms. Butler. They been waiting all morning for the practice match between North and the Academy.

For a second, I imagine what Smush would say if he could see me now, decked out in my own gear, ready to bring it—

"You a hustler, cuz," says Snapper. "A mover

and shaker. A *heartberreaker!*" He starts freestyling. 'Course all the women love him when his wife shows up with their kid.

"You all right?" Ruthie asks me.

I'm distracted, thinking about everything that's happened and trying to wrap my head around—

"Hey," she nudges me. "Look at me."

I turn and see her, for real. Her eyes, her skin—all of her.

"What do you see?" she asks.

"My girlfriend?" I ask.

"Is that even a question?" she leans in close.

"I don't know—I might need some convincin'," I say, kissing her. I hear a *click* and see Ronnie taking our pic.

"Don't worry—that's for your eyes only," he says, all smiles.

"See you at the throw-in," I say to Ruthie, heading over to the fellas just to check in.

"Not if I see you first," she says back.

Jamaica Bob fist-bumps me as I ride up on Boo. "I got big money riding on you, Cole. You bringing it, right, my man?"

"Better believe it." I glance at Harper, and he has this strange look in his eye as he stares at Boo.

"You cut his hair?"

I did. "He's a polo pony now. He's all-in," I say, sliding my hand along his crew-cut mane.

He sighs, but then looks me up and down in my new duds, and nods. "Hey, you should wear this for luck," he says. He unwraps his red bandanna and ties it around my neck.

I don't say nothing, but it's a big deal. Harp don't take his bandanna off for nobody—except me, I guess.

"Just making sure you represent us too," he says when he steps back to look. He nods in approval.

I gotta say, I'm feeling pretty all right as we line up to play. Sure, my grades aren't the best—yet. But Ruthie is helping me with a few things. Math seems to be her subject. She staying in the dorms now and is one of three girls on campus. But she has permission to visit North, and on occasion I go over to the Academy. And I gotta say, the rest of the students there aren't all stuck up like I thought they might be. The Academy actually has a few POCs, though most are from other countries. Life may be way different over there, but seeing both schools together like this makes me think we might be more the same than different.

I ride out like the Generals do—poised and ready. Coach keeps saying I'm a natural, and she keeps reminding me how I can transfer over at any time. I smile and tell her I'm thinking about it—and I am—but I got a few things to accomplish at North first.

"Coltrane!" Harp yells during warm-ups. He's holding out his phone, and when I ride over, I see Mama on the screen.

"Oh, my, you're looking good, baby. You look like a model or something!" Harp has the volume all the way up, so everybody hearing.

"Gotta go, Mama. We're about to play—"

"One more thing, one more thing! I'm coming out for a visit—and not just to see you. I got a job interview—in Philly."

"Really?" I say, surprised.

"I don't want to get your hopes up too much, but it looks pretty good. Ms. Butler says I got a good shot at it—"

She's walking around, and the connection cuts in and out.

"Wait—what? You're gonna work at *my* school?"

"Train, let's go!" says Maverick. "Stop being such a mama's boy!"

The phone cuts out, and I hand it back to Harp.

"What'd she say?" he asks.

I just shrug. "I'll tell you later."

He nods, unsure. "Okay, then, get out there and show them boys what we made of."

Coming from Harp, that's high praise. He's been spending time over at North after school, helping out. He knows his horses, and a coupla times, I caught him watching polo videos on his phone at night. You never know, maybe he got some cowboy polo in his future, especially if we ever take over the police barn and end up moving in.

"All right, time for a scrimmage," Coach shouts. "Take your positions!"

Bandit sees my red bandanna. "Still a cowboy . . ."

"You know it. To the end."

We line up, and Coach shouts, "Game on!" She throws the ball in. Bandit is quick to control it, and he and Maverick play their two-man game like they were made for it. They score pretty easily.

But on the next possession, I look to turn the ball and do a perfect hook and pull, stealing it from Maverick and sending the ball flying up to my number one. I break away and leave Maverick in my dust as I charge downfield, looking for a passback.

I hear a yell: "Yo! Nearside open!" and turn to see the ball slide on by me, within reach. Maverick sees it too, and the race is on. But I ain't gonna let him beat me. Me and Boo get the jump on them, and I'm steaming ahead—nothing but the goal and their number three, Ruthie, waiting for me.

The ball bounces and comes to a stop ahead. I raise my mallet high and straight like Ruthie showed me and bring it down smooth as silk.

I connect with the ball, sending it sailing toward the goal.

Everything feels like it's in slo-mo. I can see Ruthie's face light up as the ball flies past her—and, even though she's on the other team, she's proud to see me do my thing. My teammates raise their sticks like it's going in, but one thing I know for sure—there's no guarantees in life. Maybe I won't ever join the Academy or make it to college. Maybe the Misfits will never become state champions. Maybe Mama won't move to Philly.

Maybe me and Ruthie won't last.

But for now it's all good. The ball is heading in the right direction, and all I can do is wait to see what happens.

ACKNOWLEDGMENTS

Sometimes you put a book out into the world, and it takes on a life of its own. *Ghetto Cowboy* was one of those books that just kept on going, year after year. What started off as a story inspired by the real-life black urban cowboys of Fletcher Street in North Philly soon revealed that there were black cowboys everywhere I toured: New York, DC, Chicago, Los Angeles, St. Louis, Houston, Memphis, Baton Rouge, Tampa, and everywhere in between. The book kept getting picked up by schools, and every new class became a new set of readers. Then, miraculously, nine years after it came out, it was made into a movie called *Concrete Cowboy*, starring Idris Elba and Caleb McLaughlin, which we shot on the actual locations that inspired Chester Avenue. The real people who inspired the characters were on set every day, talking with the actors and sometimes even acting in the movie.

Meanwhile, kids kept asking when I was going to write a sequel. "I don't do sequels," I'd say, and besides, I'd need another story to write about! One of those kids said, "I know what you should write about," and proceeded to tell me about the only African American polo team in the United States, which also happened to be in Fairmount Park in Philly. I'd learned about them when I started writing the first book, but it was a totally different world, so I'd soon moved on. But the more I thought about it after, the more I couldn't stop thinking about a kind of *West Side Story* tale between two teens from different worlds—in this case, the cowboy world and the polo world. Many years passed and I wrote many versions before this one you are holding right now.

I am grateful to everyone who helped along the way:

e.E. Charlton-Trujillo, who pushed me and kept on my case long after I'd given up.

Christopher Coger-Alexander, who was the kid who reminded me about the polo team and a cowboy who played polo in Philly, and Kareem Rosser, who set the example of someone who came from nothing and became everything, all through the king of sports, polo. And my cousin Gail Ruffu, of *Grand Theft Horse* fame, for keeping it real.

Ricky Staub and Dan Walser, the filmmakers whose company, Neighborhood Films, is adjacent to Strawberry Mansion and who'd already filmed the cowboys of Fletcher Street in a way that captured them in all their glory. When given the chance to do their first feature, they picked my book, *Ghetto Cowboy*, as it represented everything they wanted to talk about in North Philly. Idris Elba, for coming aboard and making the movie happen. And the amazing producers, cast, and crew, who worked for almost nothing to bring it to life.

Karen Shafer and the kind folks at the artists colony Aunt Karen's Farm, for putting me up on their wonderful acreage in upstate New York so I could stage one last attempt at this story that kept eluding me.

Tonja Johnson and the teen readers of the Beautifully Unblemished Vitiligo Support Group for opening themselves up to me and offering their feedback. You are all beautiful.

My team on both books: Andrea Tompa, my amazing editor, who's stuck with me for all these years and saw the saga through to the end. Jesse Joshua Watson, my homie and the artist who captured these worlds so beautifully. Everyone at Candlewick Press who helped bring this story into the world, including Pamela Marshall and Hannah Mahoney for their many copyedit insights, Lauren Pettapiece for her design expertise, and Sarah Chaffee Paris and Martha Dwyer for their proofreading catches. And as always, Edward Necarsulmer IV, my agent and champion.

To all the black cowboys and cowgirls of Philadelphia and elsewhere, for inspiring my stories whether you knew it or not. You are the real deal and an inspiration to many, especially me. To Isa Shahid for keeping it 100.

And finally, my family. I literally could not do it without you.

G. NERI is the author of many books for young readers, including *Yummy: The Last Days of a Southside Shorty*, a Coretta Scott King Author Honor Book, as well as *Ghetto Cowboy*; *Hello, I'm Johnny Cash*; and *When Paul Met Artie: The Story of Simon & Garfunkel*. His books have been translated into multiple languages in more than twenty-five countries. Despite being a writer and not a rider, he has found that horses keep sneaking into his stories, perhaps because he comes from an extended family of horse people. And he is a cowboy in spirit, roaming the rugged frontiers of the world, from the jungles of Florida to the icy wastelands of Antarctica.

JESSE JOSHUA WATSON is the illustrator of many books for young readers, including the *New York Times* best-selling Hank Zipzer series, written by Henry Winkler and Lin Oliver, and *Ghetto Cowboy* and *Chess Rumble*, both written by G. Neri. In addition to writing and illustrating books, exhibiting fine art, and teaching art to kids, Jesse Joshua Watson plays music occasionally and soccer religiously. He also surfs the chilly Pacific Northwest waters as often as he can, which, as you probably guessed, is not nearly enough. He lives with his wife and sons in Washington State.